New Testaments

"Gilb's familiar signature intimacy brings us face to face with marginal housing, gritty and exhausting jobs, street people, sex, earthquakes, fouled air, physical handicaps, racism. We enter the construction world of the hired-and-fired, low pay and risky side deals to eke out meagre paychecks. Some of the stories are sidewinders: at first they indicate layers of something juicy and sweet but turn out to pierce the reader with painful splinters of insight. Vivid portraits are stitched through with slangy pocho border Spanglish. Several stories have extra dimensions, especially the surrealist punch in 'Two Red Foxes' which reminds us of the photographs of Raúl Cañibano. *New Testaments* is an enjoyable work of high craftsmanship by a notable American writer."

—**Annie Proulx**, author of "Brokeback Mountain" and *The Shipping News*

"No one writes like Dagoberto Gilb! I loved these energetic, soulful, and hilarious stories that by the end had me wondering if I'd encountered the sublime on the page."

—**Kali Fajardo-Anstine**, author of *Woman of Light* and *Sabrina & Corina*

"So alive, so wise, so gritty, sensual, so felt, so many flashes of startling poetry. I kept thinking, I've never encountered a voice quite like this one, it has this reverb that hooks you, that vibrates under the printed words and inside your own blood, what is that? But now I understand: it's pure mastery, truth, beauty, life, it's that *power,* inside this intimate space of a story but that goes on and on and never stops. Dagoberto Gilb is an American great."

—**Francisco Goldman**, author of *Monkey Boy: A Novel*

"From the first line, Dagoberto Gilb's new story collection captivates readers as if drawn by a perfectly taut silver thread. From one story to the next, each so efficient not a sentence is wasted, readers are swept through youth's most tantalizing, shining shards of memory until, inescapably, the sandstorms of time render Gilb's characters and their recollections with increasing texture and complexity. By the end, Gilb has fully immersed us in the rich amber depths where pure voice and thought become material, and time, for those precious instants, holds its breath. Dagoberto Gilb again proves to be a masterful mason of literary craft and a foundational storyteller in Chicano and American literature."

—**Carribean Fragoza**, author of *Eat the Mouth That Feeds You*

New Testaments

STORIES

Dagoberto Gilb

CITY LIGHTS BOOKS / SAN FRANCISCO

Cover art and design by Jeffrey Mellin
Text design by Patrick Barber

Library of Congress Cataloging-in-Publication Data

Names: Gilb, Dagoberto, 1950– author.
Title: New testaments / Dagoberto Gilb.
Description: San Francisco, CA ; City Lights Books, 2024.
Identifiers: LCCN 2024011686 (print) | LCCN 2024011687 (ebook) | ISBN
    9780872869318 (paperback) | ISBN 9780872869325 (epub)
Subjects: LCGFT: Short stories.
Classification: LCC PS3557.I296 N49 2024 (print) | LCC PS3557.I296
    (ebook) | DDC 813/.54—dc23/eng/20240325
LC record available at https://lccn.loc.gov/2024011686
LC ebook record available at https://lccn.loc.gov/2024011687

City Lights Books are published at the City Lights Bookstore
261 Columbus Avenue, San Francisco, CA 94133
citylights.com

Though little seen
we do exist
not for them
not because of them
For us
as us
Our lives
Our stories

These stories have appeared in the following literary journals and
online magazines:

"Answer": *Alta Journal*, Spring 2020
"Brindis at Covadonga": *A Public Space*, Winter 2022
"Peking Ducks" as "May 17, 1974": Zyzzyva.org, Summer 2023
"Prima": *Alta Journal*, Winter 2024
"The Ceiba" [an earlier version] as "Leña": *Zyzzyva*, Fall 2015
"The Dick, Casillas": Air/Light, Winter 2021
"Two Red Foxes": *Zyzzyva*, Winter 2021
"Wilshire & Grand": *Zyzzyva*, Summer 2019

CONTENTS

Gray Cloud on San Jacinto Plaza

I WAS NINE OR TEN. MY SISTER LILY WAS AROUND SIX and my sister Rosy five, and I do remember clearly that they were both wearing matching pink dresses and too shiny black shoes mom bought at Fox Plaza, an old mall nobody went to near La Jeff where, she always said, on sábados they had the best pulga with the best finds. They wore new white socks too. They had matching colas that I think were tied by ribbons but could be other little girl thingies. They were happy all the time except when they got in a whose-was-whose fight. Mostly they got along with each other great, and that day I say they were especially happy. I don't know why I don't remember anything my mom ever wore. Yes I am certain it wasn't the same cada día. She washed all ours a lot and there had to be her clothes in the piles too. My dad wore jeans and a short-sleeve shirt every day, and this day was like any. For work it was usually a T-shirt, but he also liked cotton ones with buttons, colored stripes or squares, no tails, untucked. He was wearing one of those that day. He had nice boots and work boots—he was a rock mason—but this day I say it was sneakers. Me, I don't remember. I had clothes on though.

It wasn't a Sunday. We didn't always go to Mass, but mom told me we were good Catholics, and I took her word for it especially on the good part. All three of us kids were baptized at Guadalupe Church on Alabama. Mom and Dad did get married in a church—b&w photographic evidence, my dad in a dark suit and my mom, all pretty, in a white dress with a veil—but I never wondered or asked where or who was there. I say that day in '77 or '78 was a Saturday. My parents said it might have been a weekday because sometimes my dad went on unemployment back then. It was a happy day though, because I remember well how my sisters were. And me, to me, I'm always me, but I was not unhappy for sure. We were at the edge of San Jacinto Plaza. At the northwest corner to be exact. That I remember exactly. San Jacinto was where most of the downtown city buses came and went. I especially loved them when I was younger. I also liked the plaza fountain because they said there used to be alligators in it and there was a chance they were going to put them back in there again. Pretty thrilling past and future to me. Though I don't remember how we got there or how we got home, it wasn't by bus. None of us has any memory of why we were there right then or of any practical thing we did right after, like going home. That day, that Saturday or whatever, began what was like another time frame.

The gray cloud came silently. Or it sucked all sound into its quiet, or made it detour. Turn off. Not a bird chirp, a tire squeal, a bus engine blast, a baby whimper, a dog yap, not a footstep. It wasn't hotter or colder. It didn't seem to be driven by any wind. It came toward us from where it could be Texas or Mexico or New Mexico, from that desert. The closer it got, the more it seemed we were moving toward it. From a distance, while it approached, it looked like a huge ball. But it was just gray air or gas or dust, a cloud, a cloud that blocked seeing anything in it or beyond it. Once we were all caught inside it, I felt like I had no breath. Or it was just that I was holding my breath. I couldn't see my mom or dad or sisters or anyone. I still think dad must have said *no se muevan* but I could have imagined that or even heard someone else say it. But I didn't move, as the voice I heard, or didn't really, warned me. I don't know how long this lasted. It couldn't have been many minutes. It had to be a lot of seconds because I couldn't hold my breath long enough. I remember trying not to breathe deep when I had to. And then it was over, like a light switch turned on. An off-on blink. We were at the northwest corner of the San Jacinto Plaza, exactly. Where the buses never stopped, but had. There was color again. Red and blue, yellow and green. Startling, like they'd been cleaned. My sisters were still in their pink dresses holding Mom. I cannot remember if they were sobbing or not. I think that's something that matters, but the truth is I just don't remember.

My dad, later, pronounced that it was from Asarco, the copper smelter that was in the direction of where the gray cloud came from, to the plaza and us. To me, Asarco was a giant red pipe stuck in the ground in the desert. My dad was told there was an article in the newspaper. I didn't know then that he didn't read. I mean I never saw him read anything ever, and I never thought to ask if he didn't or couldn't. Though my mom liked celebrity gossip magazines in English and Spanish, we didn't get the morning or afternoon paper. Some more days later my tía gave my mom a section of a paper that had a small box about the gray cloud that passed through the center of the city. I was excited to see it because it was something from

3

my life that made it into a newspaper. There wasn't much. A very small box that could fit in a wallet, in one of the folded sides. It said nobody knew what it was, and there were no reports of harm done, and Asarco said it wasn't anything caused by them.

It didn't matter what the newspaper said, it was a big deal in our house. We talked about it a lot. What it was like coming. What it was like inside it. What it was like after. What damage it could or might do was in our rooms a long while. Any cough or upset stomach could be because of it. Bad sleep. A bad poop. My pops finally didn't like my mom bringing it up all the time after a while, but he couldn't stop her. Not that he tried very hard. He didn't. More like, ya con eso, but not loud, not demanding. No exclamation marks. He didn't say anything, to me or us or out loud anyway, but I saw him listening whenever it came up, and I heard her get softer, shorter about it. He got that from her, she went on less for him. Me, I felt pretty much the same about it, bad or nothing but done, ya. It happened, I'm here, whatever. My sisters seemed the most affected. They'd get to babbling. Like, Mami, do you think that it might...anything...might make our hair gray like buelita's but too early, like before we get to middle school? That happened to a boy at Crockett, where I was going, like them. The boy had nothing to do with the gray cloud. Except his hair change was some months after it, and so maybe. The cana grew on a side of his head. Or like, was the reason why the zancudos didn't bite them, like they did all over to their best friend Julie next door, was that because of...the cloud? It went like this in our house for many, many months. Probably because of my mom. She dwelled on it the most. I think, or it seemed like it. Because even me, who I'd

4

say didn't, kind of did. Maybe because of my mom, but I can't say for sure. It wasn't talked about the same way after a while. But it was there without words, without having to bring it up. It was always at the front of my mom's mind. We each heard it in her, saw it in moments that were supposed to be normal and usual and would have been if she wasn't...I don't know...un poco loca? We worried.

One day in the bathroom I came out of the shower. I was beginning to dry myself off. Outside the window was what I always saw: a blue sky over everything, so close it shouldn't be called sky above, while below, where on the TV shows all of us in El Paso watched, was supposed to be green lawn, shady trees, bushy hedges, delicate flowers, was the dry brown dirt where we lived. The neighbors across the street—that was as-phalt like any TV street—lived just like us except, here and there, they might have patches of grass barely growing or dying out, waiting on desert rain. My mom kept our yard free of stray grass and weeds. We had some cactuses and sage a few feet from our house in the front and visible side that didn't take any watering usually. Our only hose was in the back-yard, where an almond tree still dropped nuts, grass beneath its shade and sharing its water. But this morning my mom, a bucket of water beside her, was soaking a patch in the center of our bare front yard. She took a shovel and began digging a widening hole. I thought it had to be a grave, a burial site for a dog or a cat, both which often found meals or water near our back door, left by my mom. But the middle of the front yard? Instead it was for a strange-looking plant—the leaves thick, dull, oval-shaped and long—that she dragged down the front steps. Big, as plants go, it was not a baby tree. Still, not what went in a center of a yard that was all dirt—or even a grass one. The dusty earth, wet now, did look a richer brown. Like me at the bathroom window, my dad silently watched her from the side of his truck—he was changing the oil. Like me, I could tell he thought it was a little off too. I was there at the window so long I dried without a towel. When my pops and I were in the living room, and my mom too, he let me know to be careful about what I might say. What she told us was that it was called a flor del cielo. A señora at the YWCA, where they had a bake sale once a month, gave it to her. It was very healthy, she claimed, for all of us, for our home.

One night, some more months later, even a year, at maybe 3 a.m., those hours for sleep, I'd been having a long dream I couldn't shake. I was with some people I didn't recognize, but who I kept thinking I did. And I was supposed to drive. I didn't drive when I wasn't dreaming, even if I pretended to in my dad's truck. I was scared of getting in trouble and maybe dying in a bad wreck or killing someone else. So I forced myself awake. I must have made a noise. My mom had come. While I was dreaming she was there. She wanted to know if I was okay. She was carrying a glass of water. I was thirsty and it really tasted especially good. Of course I was okay, I assured her. It was a dumb dream. I didn't like the dream. It had nothing to do with that gray cloud, which to her...and I remember saying to her, or only to myself, *Mom, it wasn't the gray cloud,* but she wouldn't have believed me, but she wouldn't have said she didn't believe me. I was happy she was there, happy for the water, but as good as all that was...the gray cloud happened, and it lived with us. I woke up happy I had my mom. I had some friends who didn't, or some who didn't really.

* * *

6

Hard for me to believe too, it—that gray cloud—was all the time really. Years and years. I mean, since that day, holy or unholy, both or neither, never ending. A little this, and not so small that.

Lily and Rosy, always goofy little girls, grew bigger and cuter screaming and laughing too loud about whatever—normal—but enough was all sort of off, too. For instance, they collected rocks. Not really difficult to do in El Paso since they were as all around us as cactus—actually, there were a lot more rocks in the city. This interest might have been easily explained by my pops' work as a stone mason. But that's not where it came from, and they never talked to him about the rocks he worked with, and they never showed him the ones they collected either. There was no talk of them or the collection to anyone. That might have been because there was absolutely nothing unique or pretty or impressive about any one of them that any one of us, or anybody anywhere, could see. No one would have any comment to make about any one of them or about the whole of what became their collection. So we shut up. As in, at least it wasn't a sick old dog that smelled. Or snakes. But there were no words that might sound positive or like wow, so cool. They weren't even about being pretty. They would, in fact, even be called ugly rocks. The girls didn't collect them for their size either. They ranged from small, a few smaller than a marble, and went up to various hand sizes, and a few almost big enough to be for a stone wall...though not an El Paso wall. The girls seemed to avoid those. The upper limit of size was entirely about what they could carry to their bedroom, and of course sizes increased as they got older and stronger. I offered to carry one once. Whoa, did I get an extreme no. Worse, it was like I disrupted their private play, or whatever you'd call it. For like a week I swore they avoided me. No, they never had dolls. I mean, of course a little stuffed rabbit, monkey, tiger, doggie. It's true I didn't know what girls were supposed to collect. I knew about boys, even if only a few friends. But ugly rocks? Not even boys. And the girls talked to them. Whispered between themselves and maybe to the rocks. No idea what or why. If they answered. I asked my mom and she told me to leave them alone. My dad, he was just tired, drinking a beer, falling asleep. I never asked him about his or their rocks from one day to the next.

My mom cared for her plant in the middle of the dirt front yard. She even added one more. It was kind of like an altar she'd made. She might take two buckets of water. The little circle of fertile soil in the dirt was itself a thing to stare at. In the beginning, the plants didn't seem to be dying, but it didn't seem like they were bursting with growth either. A little red popped out of the first one. A tiny tail of yellow. Mom would worry if she might miss a day tending to it, to them. She had to be home every day. In the winter and fall, it wasn't about the water but the cold. She found blankets. She went to them daily, looked in at night, checked in the morning. I wouldn't say always at the exact same hour, but it was close.

My dad was often too tired according to my mom. He told her he worked hard, that it was hard work every day even when it was an easy day. I knew that was true because every once in a while—every other year or so—I'd go out with him to a job. Younger I couldn't do a thing really. Get string for lines. In my teens I tried the chisels and hammers. The big rocks were heavy to carry and move, but what bothered me even more was how my hands got like sandpaper, wet or dry. Too much for me! That dirt and mud he showered off, but tired and sore in his muscles was his explanation for drinking beer when he got home (and there at work too, I saw that). At least a six-pack after work. More when the summer was scorching hot—months—and the crew tried to start at 5:30 a.m. He told mom that his working was why we lived well in our nice home. My mom would just look at him like she could. She didn't accept what he said. We were all in that cloud together. And she'd tell him he had to be more careful. I thought he was tired because he really was from his work. But she finally made him go to the doctor, and went with him. The doctor told them that my dad had to stop drinking so much, his liver wasn't going to able to take it, and definitely he couldn't take the amount of Tylenol and Excedrin he was. There were all these numbers as proof. He had to eat better, more vegetables. More numbers from graphs. My mom told us that the doctor didn't think any of it was because of…she didn't say because of what happened because my dad had told her, demanded, that she stop it, he couldn't take it. It'd been years already that she hadn't—at least to me and dad. Still, what she told me and my sisters right then, when dad had stepped away from the family table, is that a doctor didn't know why he was the way he was. He couldn't. He was a doctor, but he couldn't see what he can't recognize. Like what happened. How could he know? And dad started getting too tired right after, she insisted. I saw my dad standing not that far from us, out of the bathroom. He heard what she said. He listened with the same wonder we had, if she was right, if she was okay.

We stopped eating flour tortillas. My dad loved them, I loved them. Thick, fluffy, hot, soft ones were the best to me. But mom wouldn't buy them now. She bought nixtamal, two tortilla presses, a comal for the stove, and we ate fresh corn tortillas. Like they did en México, she told us. My sisters, teenagers, loved this, and their loud giggling came back to the house—maybe the rock era ended right then too—and together they patted and pressed and cooked the tortillas for every dinner. And our dinner changed. We couldn't eat carne, sirloin steak that Dad demanded every day! We ate more tacos con vegetables—chayote, pimientas of every color, calabaza, onions, cabbage. We still got chunks of pork and chicken and steak too, and we all thought our new food was good. My sisters especially. Now they were in another secret society that only our family—our grandma lived two houses away and ate with us some days too—knew about. Like they, and we, were living in a real México, not El Paso. Sometimes I swore they would dress like we were from an old Mexican movie, in long colored skirts and white cotton blouses. Not that my dad was all in, didn't want more the way it was. On a few Sundays he'd invite work buddies over, mom's sister and brother the priest and cousins, and he'd fire up the grill and it was all sirloin and burgers, charred corn and jalapeños. Or after a long Saturday job bring home pollos asados. He and I ate like mad dogs and my mom, she didn't stop the meat, only the twelve-packs of beer, not battling a six-pack, some fun.

I thought things seemed pretty good for a while there, that the gray cloud was getting past us. But no. My mom wasn't satisfied enough with her flor del cielo altar in the middle of the front yard. By then it had even become way loud—hot-rod red, yellow, and purple, light-bulb blue and Christmas green, its muscular leaves, stiff like cactus—while everything around was limp, dull fuzz, fading brown & white. A good Anglo teacher of one of the girls said it was twice the color and size of a bird of paradise, as brilliant and exotic as parrots—macaws he said—from Guatemalan jungles, where he'd been. It was as if things might be making sense, that somehow, she had seen ahead, she did something way different, changed us, battled against...whatever I mean, it made us better, or different in a good way.

Until she started telling my sisters and me that the trees in our neighborhood were struggling and she wasn't sure yet what to do about it. It reminded me of my sisters' rocks. She began walking across the street with buckets of water for the agaves that were in a neighbor's yard. It was a house no one lived in for years by then. My dad told her that cactuses have always survived in the desert without her, but she said there just wasn't enough rain, and that house was aching because its plants were dying of thirst. In the alley she found a dog dying with two broken legs, a cat barely moving that had lost an ear in a no-win fight. She didn't think anyone was caring what happened to anything. And there was more, but by then I wasn't always there in the house. The years had passed. My sisters were still there. My sisters always, always felt the same, helped like mom's thinking was their religion, something to be listened to carefully. I never went to Guadalupe Church now. My dad did on holidays, my sisters and mom every Sunday, even though mom might say that the Church didn't know enough anymore.

She'd started saying things. Like, stepping out onto our porch to look straight ahead into the night sky that rose from the horizon. The moon above might be full or less, or not visible at all. I'd say it was nice, but it was just nighttime. She'd tell me and my sisters—Dad was almost always asleep, the TV on though he never even watched a thing really—that we had to see it closer. Like a step closer? I'd ask. At the color, she said. I would tell her it was black. She, and of course my sisters, must have been two steps closer. They seemed to see more than color.

One night I really did love being at home, goofy and kooky as all my family was. I didn't live there anymore, only came once every week or two, usually to at least say hi to Mom. I don't know why this night was so perfect from the first moment. It was a delicious dinner. By this time I really appreciated the homemade and fresh tortillas the most, and our healthy food—almost vegetarian—seemed not only cool but way ahead of its time. Maybe my special happiness was because I had met a girl at UTEP. She was from Mexico. Real México, not like our house's version. I hadn't told anyone about her. I couldn't believe I could keep her, that she would want me around. I didn't even let myself hear my feelings. My dad had gone to sit by the TV for his pre-bedtime sleep. My sisters were washing the dishes. They'd told mom to go be with me because I was going to have to leave. We sat on the front porch. It was dusk, the sun almost gone, a breeze that anyone anywhere would love to feel. My mom's huge flor del cielo patch was in our view, rocks from the old collection now circling the altar, and we could see the lights twinkling over on the other side of the border. And then she told me to listen. I half smiled because I was trying to think of something teasy, smartass to say but couldn't. There was no sound. No cars, no train or whistle, no motorcycles, no kids playing or cussing, no radio too loud, not a door opening or closing. There were a few small birds singing, and a grackle. The breeze in the desert dinged a chime in somebody's yard. I'd never heard it before. We could barely hear the TV keeping my tired dad asleep. Then mom told me that silence was God's voice. I laughed. I thought of dad's snoring ignoring God. She said that when it was this quiet, we could hear and see God. I couldn't think of anything sarcastic to say to that. It seemed impossible to talk at all. Then Lily came out the door, Rosy right behind. The dishes were all done.

* * *

Let me say that it wasn't just them. I was not so...reckless after the gray cloud. Where I was bothered, when, why, how, well I will just say it was after the gray cloud that it seemed to begin. My dad got tired all the time, anytime. My sisters got secretive, cultish, wary of others. My mom...call it what you will. Me, what I did was live in my bedroom like an ascetic monk. Or a weirdo freak. I had a bed, a blanket, two pillows. The blankets and pillows were like my girlfriends. I loved them truly. I didn't even like my mom messing with them for normal purposes. Although clean pillowcases and a clean fitted sheet were fine, good even. No bedspread, no top sheet. I made no bed ever. I had a desk, which once in a while had a book on it, but never more than two. From the library or a textbook. I didn't do all my homework. I'd pick and choose. No chair. Work was while laying on my stomach on my bed. I had a lamp. I had nothing on the walls. Nothing. No Jesus or bizarro rocker or hot fantasy babe. I did listen to music. At the Fox pulga, way back when, my mom got me a boombox. It didn't boom, and I didn't have cassettes, I just kept it on KLAQ pretty low a lot. So only I could hear. It was on the table, which was also near the lamp and my bed. I'd eventually started playing sports and I made friends. They could never come over because I would never invite them. I was good at track (the mile) and baseball (second base, batted second) and basketball, though I never started even as a senior. Nobody heard about the gray cloud and its consequences from me.

I studied Spanish not because we lived in the México of my mom's creation, but because I lived in El Paso, Texas. I liked learning to be good in Spanish. We'd grown up with it around and in my mom and dad, but it wasn't like it was necessary to speak Spanish except around our buelita. It is only coincidental that I decided to make it my career when she died. And that had nothing to do with any gray cloud.

Lily didn't want to go to college and she met a boy. It was true love. Everyone wanted the works. A way expensive white gown. He would wear a charro suit. It would be at Our Lady of Guadalupe Church. The priest would be my uncle, my mother's brother, Guillermo Cordero. The reception would have 200 (his side mostly) invited, and my mom would do all the cooking except the dessert and a fabulous tiered wedding cake. An open bar but with lots of aguas frescas—my mom would make her horchata. Flowers were to be in excess, especially lilies and roses too. There were mariachis hired. There was a DJ hired. There was a limousine hired. A pro photographer and videographer. It was so exciting that my dad didn't seem too tired. And Lily's fiancé's family was well off, and they wanted to pay for it all.

Lily died ten days before the ceremony. There were no warning symptoms. Her heart stopped in the middle of the night, early morning. Nothing diagnostically wrong, it just quit beating. My mom collapsed in tears for a week. My dad tried to stay awake more but he still worked on rock walls six days a week—he was a foreman then. Rosy went between rolling sobs and blank stares for months. My mom mourned for six months. She would go to the church on Sunday but sometimes she would turn around and go home and water her flowers from heaven, sit there. She didn't notice people who'd be a few feet from her. Or she would react quickly to people who said anything to her but not be able to talk. With us it was more like *you know*.

It was not eight months later that my dad died. He was asleep in his chair, that TV on. He was too young too. Not even sixty yet. They said it was heart disease, liver damage, lung damage, all damage that explained his exhaustion. But he wasn't fat. He was even lean, ripped in no-gym workout ways, from hard work, from years of eating Mom's good food and not drinking so much beer. He looked a decade younger than all the men his age, and he could outwork the youngest stone mason.

And not two weeks later my mom died. Rosy and I didn't even know she was older than dad because she'd lied to us...you could take her for a woman in her early thirties from a distance. Rosy found her with her head on the family table. Like she'd been crying.

Rosy thought that mom had been right all along. Rosy felt bitter. I said it could be lots of things too. Rosy said we had to be strong. I said we were strong. She said we had to be stronger. I said we could make sure we were happy. That she had to be happy. She didn't think she knew how to now. I told her she could. I meant someone, something, besides Lily and besides mom. To think how dad and mom loved each other, that was pretty great. Rosy and I really hadn't talked much all these years. And I'm not saying we talked very well or clearly to each other this first night after so much.

Only a few years later I was married to Valentina, the mexicana I fell so in love with. I was translating, both directions, for government and lawyers and business people. We didn't have to live in El Paso. We bought a house in Mexico City, in Coyoacán, on Calle Xicoténcatl. It had five bedrooms and bathrooms, a roofless jardín in the center of the structure. I had so much work, we did—Valentina did this work too—that one day a week I could write letters for ordinary people to a distant mother or father, son or daughter, all kinds. It was my favorite work of all, and I didn't charge much, only enough for them to feel I was professional. Valentina, pregnant, had plants everywhere—we couldn't find flores del cielo, but many birds of paradise. She hung paintings, art, on every wall, even in our bedroom where she was better than any pillow or blanket. And that was when Rosy came to live with us. Now she and I giggled and, though these weren't secrets, we were alien citizens, and we'd come from a world far away and long ago, and as often as possible we listened to the silence.

Brindis at Covadonga

IN THE STATES HE DIDN'T EVEN LIKE TO TELL PEOPLE he was born in Mexico City, because it always seemed to bring up, to them, all sorts of images and assumptions that had nothing to do with his actual life and memories of growing up in East Hollywood. His LA was Armenians, Turks, Lebanese, Filipinos and Thai and Cubanos, Blacks, Mexicanos, and Chicanos. Also aging and old white people who all seemed to wear funny hats. Lots of drunks and enough tecatos. On the streets too many prostitutes and homeless and people in wheelchairs. Nobody rich or close to it. Lots of fire trucks and ambulances, police cars and helicopters.

Samuel spoke Spanish like maybe a sixth-grader, English like a high school dropout who got Ds and Fs. Which he got and was. But eventually he did all right. He got a great maintenance job in the nearby hospital where his mom was a housekeeper too, and he became the department's supervisor. He worked easy with everyone, married, bought a house, fathered two children, divorced, sold the house and let a judge split the gains and losses. He took the pension when it was a deal to retire, and now he wasn't young anymore. His children didn't live in LA. One was in the military, still in Afghanistan, the other, already three babies, was in Denver. They needed every-thing but him.

Samuel had come to Mexico City over two weeks ago. He wasn't sure why he came, but thought he might stay a while. It was more of a why not than because. The few people he called friends, people he barely spoke to much, if ever—he had time, they didn't—all of them said he was going home. He resisted mocking that, as tiresome as it was. One longtime friend—he only knew him from work—who was always very hippie-wise because he'd gone to college and so what he didn't finish, said that lots of animals go back to their 'natal birthplace' to die. Samuel's first reaction was to cuss him and hang up for good. Let *him* die. The man had been this same exact, deeper-than-thou jerk forever. That and a few more explained why Samuel had bcome his boss, while he still carried screwdrivers around.

Samuel was on his way to see his sister-in-law, Flor, his older and only brother's smart Oaxacan wife. When he first met her, she was still called an *india*. Zapoteca. She was not, like these brothers, mestizo, mixed. Roby went crazy for her, everything about her, and everything she believed in—so it seemed to Samuel. Roby was born Roberto. Once their mother moved them all to the States, the schools made him Robert. To everybody else, Robbie. He went back to *la capital* often—unlike Samuel, he missed it, and traveled back when-ever he could, staying with grandparents and friends he made growing up. He was good at art, talented, and then he met Flor. There he became Roby—not pronounced like a robber but a rower—and now she preferred to be called an *indígena*. By his later twenties, he never came back to the States—ex-cept for trips to New York—even to see his mom (their dad had abandoned them early along). She went to see them often when Roby and Flor had babies. Though she never accepted the invitation to live with them. Roby's art sold in Europe and China, and they seemed to be living well. Art was everywhere in their home, canvases leaning, hanging, stacked, piled sideways, and stored in every otherwise unoccupied space. Samuel couldn't go to visit much if at all because of his work—which didn't pay enough for trips either—and he didn't really want to because he always felt out of his element. Like Roby and Flor were from a faraway, better, and more exotic land than where he was raised. His brother was both more native and worldly, one whose life was as mysterious to him as it was obvious—as bright as yellow red and blue oil paint. And then, years ago already, suddenly, he died.

* * *

Samuel never thought about taxis in the States—like he ever had a reason to—but here this luxury transportation was two or three dollars. He even learned to Uber.

"I love your wheels," he told the driver. It was a glossy black Toyota, not new, but kept in excellent condition.

The driver eyed him through the mirror. "I am sorry, but I don't understand."

"I'm sorry," Samuel said in Spanish. "I forgot where I was. All this green here. Nothing like where I live."

The driver still saw him from his rearview. "Where are you from?"

"The States. Where else?"

"Could be many countries," the driver said. "I see people from all over the world."

Samuel nodded. "It's so beautiful," he said. He still had to think of certain words and sentences before he spoke. "Like a garden...in the...I don't remember the word...where Tarzan lived...green, everywhere green green, big green plants."

"Jungle," the driver suggested.

"Yes, that's it. I can't remember so many words. Or I never knew them. The simplest ones, you know?"

The driver spoke at him through the rearview. "But you know Spanish enough."

"I was born here."

"In Mexico?"

"Yes, right here, in Mexico City." He wanted to tell him how he knew that was hard to believe, but that was too complicated. "It's so beautiful," he said again instead. "My sister-in-law told me that...that that was what the conquistadors said when they first saw it here." Samuel had gone with Flor and one of her daughters, his niece, to the Zócalo a week before for the five-hundred-year anniversary of the defeat of the Aztecs and destruction of Tenochitlán by the Spanish.

The driver listened, eyes driving, GPS guiding.

"So this is how you make a living?" Samuel asked. "With Uber? It's good? Enough?"

The driver turned his eyes into the mirror. "I've only done this for a few months now. It's not so bad. I'm sixty-seven. I couldn't find any other job. It's been very hard."

"Because you're old, or because of the pandemic?"

"The two," the driver said.

"But you have...*social security*? For your old age?"

"¿Cómo?"

"A pension," said Samuel.

The driver shook his head calmly and drove.

"Not from the government. Not from your job?"

"I worked many years, all my life," the driver said easily. "In radio and television. I loved my job. But it was always as a contractor. *Freelance* in English. And I saved nothing. The work was slowing for me and stopped over a year ago. All work. A friend told me about doing this Uber."

"Radio and television. Wow. That's good work. You have to know...things. Smart things." He thought about how little this trip was costing. "And now Uber."

The driver told Samuel names of the TV and radio programs he'd worked for. Samuel knew none, but they were all clearly well known in the city and maybe country—the driver's pride glowed in the mirror, even though his voice stayed even, calm. Another person might have turned and looked right at Samuel when he mentioned one name, a star or famous host he'd worked for the longest.

Samuel responded spontaneously. "How great is that?" he said, no idea of who or what.

"A long time," the driver told him. "I never thought..."

"I'm lucky," Samuel said, "because I didn't either."

* * *

Samuel and Flor were going to visit a realtor about a foreclosed house in San Ángel. He didn't know anything about these matters, but Flor thought that his presence might add somehow. She said she loved her home, their family home for so many decades, but maybe it would be best if she sold it and left. Things were bad for everyone these days. But if she could get that house, that property, for that price they were quoting...though she didn't want to move. It just seemed smarter if she did. Samuel didn't think to ask if she was in trouble somehow. His brother had always seemed rich to him.

As Samuel was waiting to pass through the wrought-iron gate after he'd buzzed her, a man, dressed well, came out the door. Flor's dog was going wild deciding which man was more important. As Samuel walked inside, Flor's two cats both came to him like dogs wanting to smell.

"I thought he would take two or even three more paintings to sell," she said.

"And instead he wanted...directions, or maybe a date?"

She didn't go along. "They're not selling."

"Roby's paintings?"

"It's a bad day," she said.

He waited a bit for her. Then, "But you still want to go?"

"Yes, we will go."

He petted a cat and the dog at the same time. It was unnaturally quiet, not usual.

She offered him coffee and warmed some for them both and sat at the table across from him.

"Don Emiliano died today," she finally said.

He couldn't register what she was telling him.

"He drove us. Everywhere, all the time. That man."

"The taxi driver? The one you always...every time I've ever been here. A couple of days ago."

"He was more part of our family. He even knew my mother."

"I remember him from all the years back," Samuel said again.

Flor didn't seem to have much more to add.

"When?" asked Samuel.

"This morning. His son called me an hour ago."

They sipped the coffee.

She said, "Do you know that today is the anniversary of Roby's death?"

Samuel didn't say no but didn't have to.

"He died here on this day. He didn't want to go to the hospital to die. He wanted it to be here, with us."

Samuel had come for the funeral, but there was much he didn't know. "Well, I don't think we should go today. It is a bad day, like you told me."

"I can go," Flor said. "We have the appointment."

"I don't think we should. We shouldn't go. Not today."

She agreed. She called to postpone.

"I can leave, too," Samuel said. "Maybe you have other things, or you want to be alone, or..."

"No no, stay. You can stay. We can have cena as we planned. Something here, or maybe good to go out."

"Whatever you say," he said. "What's best for you."

"I know where we want to go," said Flor after a few moments.

* * *

A random taxi drove them at the beginning of the evening's rain. It was a light drizzle, almost a mist, and it made everything seem shaded and lush, a tropical green. The restaurant was the Covadonga. Samuel remembered going there with both Roby and Flor, and also with Roby alone, though he was never alone, especially here. Everybody knew him, and he knew everybody. The entrance canopy that reached all the way to the street, with its coat of arms and logo and even a doorman, was more New York than Mexico. It saved them from getting wet. Up a few stairs they entered a huge hall, a Mexican cantina bigger than any of those you see in American

Western movies. So many tables, for whatever the party size, generously spread around, tablecloths and folded, pressed napkins, dinnerware sparkling, TVs on the wing side walls, a long wooden bar at the far end. But the Covadonga's cantina style wasn't of a dusty charro era of horses and broad sombreros, haciendas and Pancho Villa. It was from the forties and fifties, when cars were heavy and slow, waiters dressed like French officers, the Spanish food was for the higher class.

"When I come here I think of happy times," Flor told Samuel.

"It's pretty great," he said. "I remember one really fun night drinking too much here."

"Loud and noisy, busy," she said. "Singing and laughing. Gritos. Happiness."

A waiter came and she greeted him by his first name. He called her Doña Flor. They both talked about it being too long. She ordered a gin and tonic. Samuel ordered a beer, but the label's *especial* just to be a little more classy than he was.

"What a good idea," he told her.

The drinks arrived with a formal grace.

"*Un brindis,*" Flor pronounced. She raised her glass. "To Don Emiliano. My whole family loved him. I loved him, and I will miss him."

They clinked and sipped.

"To Roby," Samuel said, his beer glass forward, "and to your love for him."

Again they clinked and sipped.

"To México," she said before he relaxed, "and for the five hundred years before, too." That was for them to smile.

Some friends from a table across the restaurant approached her, and then she went to their table for a while to speak to an elderly man and came back.

"He is at least a hundred years old, even more. He always seemed as old as México. Of course he knew Emiliano, too. So small our world. His older sister was the one who first took him in. Don Emiliano was eleven and he wore mismatched shoes and he wanted a job, any job whatever. He never wanted to go back to what was supposed to be his home. He would never drink. And he always worked more than anyone to raise his family," she said.

They didn't wait long for their food. She got a bean stew from Asturias, and he got a paella from Valencia.

"Did you know that the Spaniards tortured Cuauhtémoc after they captured him? They said he was hiding gold, maybe even in his body. And here we are, choosing their food."

"But didn't you tell me that if the Aztecs..."

"*El mexica...*"

"...had it their way, we'd be eating conquistador thighs?" Samuel said. "I barely eat fish, and yeah I eat chickens and cows, but I'm not eating no Spaniard even if I want him worse than dead."

"Might be tasty. Especially in Oaxacan *mole. Con chocolate.*"

Samuel kept laughing. Hers died out.

"Ours was a culture of much natural beauty," she said. "But we fought too much among ourselves, hating each other. Cortés should never have gotten close. No one can ever know what we could have been, what we could have taught and learned from one another."

Samuel tried to keep it light. "You wish you were still bare-foot, making tortillas?"

"Well, I love *las mujeres* making *las tortillas,*" Flor told him. "I love tortillas. I love our corn. I love our earth and our rain and our sun. I am proud of us. We are the people of *esta tierra.* It isn't always easy, but *así es.*"

She waited for him but Samuel wasn't used to this talk. When the bill came, he said, "Let me buy tonight." They usually divided all evenly. "Please, it's on me."

* * *

Because it had to be a day for hard rain, it was. They'd left before the downpour, but inside Samuel's rental, rain was pud-dling through the windows or walls to the floor. He had only one towel—besides the one he selfishly kept for showering—but he didn't have three more, what it would take if it lasted too much longer. He kept his shoes on. Choosing this place was his kind of mistake—it was cheaper than that one, or that, and what great difference except the price? This was him since the beginning, who he was.

In fact the rented departamento was like his earliest mem-ories of being in México. The tiny kitchen, barely big enough for a stove, and a refrigerator that wasn't designed to be in-cluded either. The bathroom that smelled of leaky toilet. The windows with a view of the old building's tattered interior ductwork, or those on its exterior side, looking out through glass probably not washed since its installation onto a hand-some plot of vacant lot garbage dump. Faint lighting, like the mental light of his memory, like the reality of the dim bulbs hanging on their electrical wires from the ceiling holes. He didn't remember furniture, and this place, but for a sofa covered by a Mexican blanket, had none. What he remembered from his earliest childhood was how every inside space for play had its danger. That was part of whatever game they invented. He had no toys that he could remember. What he had was Robbie. He was the best toy. He was safety and light wherever there was darkness.

He turned on the large-screen TV. It was part of the sell of this place, and it was accurate. Connection fuzz and interruptions aside, he could watch a Dodger game on the deportes channel. The color on the TV, the only light, was a mural on the drab wall. He was in México. He got into bed and paid attention to the rain, after many booms of thunder and sharp strikes of lightning, until it calmed.

The trembling began slowly, but the seconds were enough for Samuel to become aware and pull on pants and slip on socks and shoes and stand. The TV blanked and then darkness. His left hand went to the wall as a guide and balance. The plaster had become plastic, molten, wavy. He grabbed up his phone. He felt it was his own anxiety making the room seem to roll up and down. He heard voices in the building's hallway and feet pounding down the stairs. The room began rocking and even in the darkness a white dust seemed to be a spray of light and he heard a large chunk of something thudding on one side of his door or the other. He decided to stand in the doorjamb he was near, his hands gripping, arms pressing either side. His eyes, watching everywhere they could, his brain preparing for a drop under him or a sudden falling from above. But it stopped. The seconds, maybe forty-five, maybe sixty, seemed long and he waited more seconds. Electricity came back and he opened his door. The chunk, window-size, was from an upper corner, his door side. The door of the departamento across was open and he walked there and looked inside and said hello hello and no one. Outside people milled about. He went back up.

The television was on again and he changed it to news. They were gathering information on the magnitude and damage. The phone rang.

"You're fine?" Flor asked him.

"I'm shaky," he said. "I don't know what to do. I've always been scared…though never the little ones I've felt in LA."

"Nothing to do," she said.

"Where are you?" he asked.

"At a wake for Don Emiliano."

"Really?…Nothing happened there?"

"It shook all, all of us. For a moment. But…I am glad I was here. I am still."

"You're not worried about your home?"

"Not enough, no. I'm sure it will be fine."

"Okay then," he said.

"Aren't you glad to be back where you're from?" she teased him.

Samuel laughed as she wanted him to.

"Thank you," he told her. "I should have come back sooner."

"You're here now," she joked. "Like you never left."

Two Red Foxes

IT WAS DRIVING HIM A LITTLE CRAZY THAT HE couldn't find the mini-mag flashlight he bought not a week ago. There were all kinds of possible explanations for it being gone, the best being that, since he still had the old one the new one was replacing, he accidentally threw out the new one instead of the old. It was his own first thought, which had become his daughter's only one once he told her that it was possible. It wasn't really though, and he didn't mean it to be taken as likely. He meant it more as something he considered as he was talking to her. He wasn't trying to talk perfectly, didn't think he had to. What he meant only, that particular day, was how he felt crazy searching and searching and not finding it.

He in fact did check all his trash everywhere, but he didn't believe for one second he threw it out. Yes, the trash outside had been collected the day before he realized it was lost, and there was that, forever where it was if he never found it. But he didn't remember taking any trash out there for at least a week before he got the new flashlight. And his old mag light was red, the new purple. He didn't throw the purple away thinking it was red. And he had trouble tossing out valuable things, what seemed valuable, well-made, like the flashlight, even if it was cheaper to get a new one than try to fix it. It'd worked so well, it looked like new. Probably just that tiny bulb. It just wasn't him to throw away quality objects. He'd looked in the garage, every inch of the cement floor, and into the mess of saws and wrenches and pliers and hammers and screwdrivers and nails and screws and bolts and old faucets and rubber washers and shower heads and tubing and cans of all sorts of sprays and gloves and shop rags and ripped-up ones and cords. It was not there both times he went through it all, or inside, for whatever impossible reason, some tool-boxes he had and where he would never have put it anyway. There were other possibilities. That he'd put in his pocket—he never did that—and he walked it to his car and it fell outside the door. Once, years ago, he almost lost a pair of sunglasses that way, but he realized it fast and drove back and there they were, on the asphalt where he'd parked. He'd only driven the car once since the mag light went missing, a short trip to a drugstore drive-thru window, and he never got out. He checked under its seats and in the seat cracks. Made no sense but he'd looked, and no. He never walked the front yard, grass high and needing a mow, too many weeds, agaves and yuc-cas and a couple sage bushes. It was a flashlight, not a nickel or even a quarter. It wasn't there. He looked there once more anyway, and it still wasn't there. Not in the car, not on the driveway, not on the turn-left route to walk two blocks to the corner store or good coffee in the morning café, not on the turn-right route to walk a few to that park and sit under shade trees for a bit in the afternoon. Not in the back yard either. Too damn hot in the back, too wild, and he should get some-one to whack it down out there and lessen the insects maybe.

Maybe tree snakes and brown recluse besides the squirrels. He saw the reddest cardinals from inside through the back picture window. And white-spotted woodpeckers. The bluest jays. One bird he didn't know but was bright purple. He loved all of them from his bed, eyes closed in the early morning, like he was inside a full birdcage. He didn't lose it out there. The back door was still and always locked. He felt like maybe he was making himself more crazy going out that door for even a few moments, moving only his eyes, then some steps around and through all the bug bites and sharp burrs. He knew he did not lose it there unless it took itself out there crawling or rolling magically on its own. It was somewhere in the house, that was the only real possibility. Although there was one other. That somebody came in and stole it. That was what his abuelita used to cry when she was in her mid-80s. Every time anything got misplaced, before it was found an hour or days later, it was, *¡me robó un pendejo!* It'd always be something like a scarf, or a handkerchief, or a big spoon, a cheap bracelet, or a five-dollar bill. That became how he thought about what it was when the brain, life, was getting bad. That somebody pocketed and snuck out with the new mini-mag flashlight could not be what happened. He was more worried because he couldn't help himself from considering that *who if?*, that thinking this way itself was already the first worm in his coffin.

When he got out of bed in the morning, he couldn't help looking over everything that he had already looked through a thousand times. It still wasn't hiding in plain sight or behind his toothbrush. Still not behind the bathroom trash can. While he peed, he almost missed the bowl, looking away yet again at that darker narrow side near the wall. Not this time either in the clutter of nothing on the chest of drawers where he kept his morning pills. He moved toward the kitchen, slower than he liked, to look, again, behind doors he passed. It was a craziness, and he so hated it. He put his not very good coffee in the too old, too slow coffee maker and poured the tap water into it and stepped to the little breakfast table—he ate dinner lots of times there—by the big picture window facing the front yard. He never sat until he had sipped some coffee.

He stared at the morning on the other side of the glass, and his eyes filled with the wonder of a child. At first he didn't believe what he saw. It shook him it was so sudden. He wasn't certain if they had been there all along, or just appeared in the corner of the window. They were two. A few heartbeats came and went. Not dogs. Another pause. Foxes. They were foxes. Yellowish red, not big but not small, that snout, those ears. They were on the driveway, from the side of the garage, must have come through the overgrown backyard. The one in front of the other was staring far ahead, across the street he lived on, alert. Seeing and hearing something? And then that fox was on its way there. Not a sprint, but a strong prancing run, toes barely touching, not hurried but quick, not straight but direct.

Excited, he went outside and onto the front yard grass to see. There was nothing to see. They weren't coming back to jump on him happy. But he had to go out. Nobody else was around. It was just as humid hot like it was all the days before, even in the mornings.

"You won't believe it," he told his daughter Tinita. "I don't believe what I saw." She didn't say anything. She waited. "Two red foxes! Is that something or what?"

"At the house?" she said.

"Yes! Outside."

"There are foxes? There?"

"I saw them," he said. "Right on my driveway. Until they ran off."

"Couldn't they be dogs?" she said. "Dogs checking the trash cans."

"They were red foxes, mija," he said deflated.

"I guess that is something," she said. "I've just never heard of it before."

"You don't believe me."

"I believe you, Daddy," she told him. "Honest."

"Sure doesn't sound like it."

There was quiet.

"Have you ever heard of coyotes in back yards?" he asked. "There have been coyotes seen down the street. There was a story recently, somewhere, in the newspaper maybe, online somewhere." He didn't tell her he thought he saw one, a baby one, in his back yard a year or two ago. He didn't tell her about it then either. "In some places, not here of course, they get bears."

She could hear he was frustrated with her. "I'm sorry, Daddy."

He was done now. "I forgot why you called."

"You called me..." she started.

"That's what I meant to say," he interrruped.

"...to tell me about the foxes, I think."

"Yeah sure, it's okay," he said to drop it. "Babies good?"

Then he heard something. A bird. Really close to a window?

"Your nietos are, but the others wear this mami out."

He took an extra second or two, listening away from her. Then back. "Still a las cinco de la mañana?" he said. "That is early."

"It's probably just that, me wanting an hour or two more. By the time they get picked up, I'm shot."

The chirping was steady.

"Well, if you gotta make the money," he said.

"I really shouldn't give it up. If it were two hours later, even one."

"So I'll let you go work."

A frantic bird.

"I love you, Daddy," she said sadly.

It seemed in the backyard, maybe at the back window, in the eaves maybe. There, the sound had stopped. No bird he could see either. He returned to the kitchen, to his coffee. The chirping came back. This time he checked a front bedroom, its window, but nowhere near. Not next at the bigger bathroom's window—the chirping was back where he thought. It stopped once he got close. He waited. And there it was again, and this time he thought he could even hear wings fluttering. It wasn't from the attached garage. In the house? Seemed like near that back window in the living room had to be it but it stopped once he was there. He opened the back door and waited, still, from inside, feeling the outdoor heat rolling past him. He listened. Nothing outside, no chirping like he'd heard.

He shut the door and there it was. Way up in a corner of what had become a spare room, bedroom, weight room, junk room, closet with a desk, his daughter's art storage and books and boxes of who-knows anymore. The ceiling was higher than normal. One window, always closed because it had been painted shut since before he lived here.

The little bird had to be a baby, it was so small. Probably a baby finch. He tried to somehow catch it. Reaching with a hand, then a hat, then a straw trash basket. He tried a dust pan to guide it to the open back door. Not a close call. It frantically flew from corner to corner and landed on whatever it could. Only the cooled AC air went out. He talked to it sweetly. That he wanted to help it get back outside. He was sure the little bird was miserably scared and all he'd managed to do was scare it more. He saw the little eyes staring, even as its beak was pointed away. He didn't know how he'd do it.

* * *

"Joe Mama!" Neto laughed like always, like this play on his name had never been said before, like he just this moment made it up fresh. "You seeing in the dark again? Or was it even in the day so you don't accidentally eat dog food instead of hamburger? Remember, one comes in a can you gotta open, the other from the frigerator. No flashlight or close up smelling necessary!"

His oldest living friend, from all the way back to first grade, Neto still lived in the neighborhood like he did. They both lived a block away from their parents' home. He hadn't talked to Neto for years until a few days ago, when he first couldn't find the flashlight. His name tease came from what all the kids called him then, Joma, because that was how it was to Anglo teachers on their class rosters instead of José María. He himself used Joe, as most did.

"So you seeing now, viejo?"

"I haven't found the dumb thing, no."

"You need to find you a young brain, that's all."

"I misplaced more shit when I was in my twenties and thirties. I just never had any time to look."

"You positive you bought it? Maybe that's the fuckup." He thought that was hilarious. "Sucks getting old."

This was why he'd stopped talking to Neto. He talked like they were old thirty-some years ago. Everything for him was downhill since they'd graduated high school.

He wasn't going to talk about the baby bird. But he told him about the red foxes, mostly to switch the subject and because, besides it being a kind of thrill, he thought Neto'd like it.

"Sounds like dogs to me," Neto said. "You sure? Maybe you needed a flashlight."

"Red foxes," he said, pissed. "Two."

"Why two?"

"¿Cómo?"

"Why not four? Or five. Like wolves."

"Like wolves?"

"Simón. That'd be más wild, no? Those ice cold ojos, you know? And a pack, you know?"

"Neto, you trying to piss me off, or you just do?"

"I'm funning with you, viejo," Neto said. "Come on, you know how I am."

"Sounds like you're saying something about me."

"Okay. You got me some there," Neto said.

"What then?"

"I never seen a fox in my life, but I don't think they travel in twos."

"How do you know that?"

"Man, I don't know. Maybe...probably a TV thingie. Not a movie like 'Dancers with Foxes'... That sounds like one to watch though, no? I'll go with do-gooder TV. Like on a Saturday. When you got a broken foot, like I had."

"You're so fucken stupid," he said.

They were both laughing a little.

"It was two."

"Been a hella picture to catch," said Neto.

He didn't say anything but what he felt came across.

"I was just thinking of old eyes, two flashlights, seeing double wolves," Neto said, laughing still. He noticed he was laughing alone. "I'm funning around, man, joking. Come on, old man. I'm only playing."

* * *

He could push the little bird out of the room and then get it into another room with windows that opened. Then again, he had to be able to catch the bird. He shut the door and did what he could. The uneven ceiling was too high at this end, even if shelves and stacked boxes it landed on weren't—it'd fly up if he got close. After only a short time he was wearing himself out and panicking the bird, who'd smacked the door, walls, ceiling, and window more than once. One time it fell to the floor and hopped until it gathered itself and flew up to a high box. He could break down all his room so there was nothing too high. He could break out the glass of the window—an excuse to fix it. He decided he'd try to trap the little bird. He got a bowl of water and some bread he broke up and piled next to it and got his straw trash basket ready nearby. It stayed quiet as long as he did.

Gonzalo was a young man from Tamaulipas who, along with his wife and three baby girls, came to live with his neighbors, the Sandovals. Cared for both of them until they passed and stayed on as renters. Gonzalo could do a lot of things, and his wife made ricas enchiladas with rice and frijoles, and one or all three of the girls would often come over with a plate for him. He had an open invitation to drop in whenever they had an afternoon cookout with friends, playing music and laughing in their yard. Much as he loved pollo and beef asados, and even though he knew they really didn't care about his dropping by like he did, he was shy about coming alone and not young like all of them.

His best idea was to ask Gonzalo to come over and catch the little bird for him because, like he knew he himself once could, Gonzalo could catch it fast and easy. And of course Gonzalo said he could do that after he got out of work. He'd found a good job at a restaurant not too far away. That night, or in the morning if that were better, it was not a problem, anything, any time he could help.

Gonzalo always called him *maestro*. That's what he loved most about *Mexican* Mexicans, that respect was in the common language and especially toward the old. It made him feel, anybody getting older, less beaten down, like age was an achievement. Mexicans from here, like Neto, made age out to be all loss.

"I think it got in when I went outside to see the foxes," he told Gonzalo. "I left my front door open."

"To see what?" Gonzalo asked him.

He struggled for the word in Spanish that maybe he never knew, so he said *los foxes*. What his kind of Mexican from this side did all the time. "You know, like a small wild dog. Like a wolf, only smaller, in a forest. The color of a coyote but more red, and smaller."

"¿Un zorro?"

"Exactly!" he cried. He'd never have thought of it ever, but he knew that was it. It made him even happier. "Two of them!"

"It's possible?" Gonzalo asked. "I have never seen a fox anywhere."

"They were in my driveway in the morning," he told him slowly. He slowed down even more remembering and telling it in Spanish. "Then they ran across the street, into the yard across from yours. That's why I went out. To see if they were there, or still moving."

"Dos zorros," Gonzalo said. "Increíble."

His excitement was like a childhood memory. But now he remembered only the one running. "From my driveway," he said again.

"They weren't dogs?" Gonzalo asked. "I see lots of dogs without owners."

"Fox," he said. "Red like fox. A nose like fox. Everything like fox." He was willfully using the singular. He was mad at himself. "We live in a type of region they are used to living in. Before all of us were here."

"Wow. That's great, maestro. I hope I get to see them, too. My daughters would too."

He wanted to say it was a one in a million thing to see one in the wild.

"So best for you early in the morning to come by for me?"

"As you say, of course. Whatever you want, maestro, I'll help you."

He hadn't heard the bird in a while and he opened the door and nothing. No movement. The bowls of water and bread seemed untouched. All things seemed both as new and not as the word *zorro*. He didn't know it, maybe he should know it, but he didn't, and yet he knew it when he heard it. It was that fox he saw. Only it was one running across the street. It wasn't two, he really didn't see two ever? He might get Gonzalo to come as soon as he got off work, whatever the time. He chirped *birdie birdie* a few times. He didn't want to upset the little bird. He didn't want it flying crazy afraid around the house, he didn't want it to die. When Gonzalo came, the two of them together, could get the little bird and free it. What else to do? It was a lost little bird, he was an old man who couldn't catch it. Nothing there new in the world.

He went to see the route the foxes might have passed by. If it was for the trash in the trash cans, which it wasn't. He was sure now. They couldn't have jumped his chain-link fence even though it wasn't considered high. Not an easy climb or leap. From that tree? And if there, not onto a cement walk but to a high mound with overgrown grass, and then from there it was a small hop down to where the cement path and trash cans were. And ahead, in the driveway...and there it was. A pile of caca. It was almost exactly where he saw the two of them from his window. Even could explain why the one he watched—he didn't know how the one became two, or the two one—was standing there as long as it did, staring, seeing not close but far. It was only a few seconds before it took off. The caca was not exactly hot fresh, but not dry either. It was not a dog's. More a blue black like a grackle's tail, with seeds, and pieces of feather in the droppings.

* * *

At dusk he opened the door of the spare room for a last check on his little lost bird. And it was there by the water bowl. Upright, it stayed completely still as the door opened. It might have eaten some of the bread on the floor. He moved gently closer and close enough, lowering himself slowly. He let his left hand reach around from its tail and he grabbed it. He could feel it then, but that didn't last. It was calm. He talked gently. They looked at each other, even if its small black eyes were aimed ahead. With his right hand he offered bread crust and it seemed to want to peck at it. He went to the back door and opened it, talking gently all the time. Went out to the lush green humidity. He squatted his legs, which wasn't that easy for old, damaged him. He set the little bird down, and it hopped a little and steadied. Shook its feathers, like a quiver. Then a couple of running steps and hops and up, and in seconds out of his sight. He felt joy like since he couldn't remember when. He went in and came back with the bowl of water, and bread, and placed them near the door and closed it.

* * *

"I'm checking up on you," his son he still called Junior, half-sarcastically between them. His son preferred his middle name, and he dropped the accent on the é in José Javier. He went by JJ to most friends since he was young. He lived in Los Angeles now. He'd lived in New York, then he was in Dallas, and then Denver.

"You're the one needs checking up on," he said.

"Why's that?"

"How old are you again? And still no grandkids, not a wife, can't even say it's a divorce. Who you shacking up with these days?"

"Same woman it's been for three years, pops."

"And I'm supposed to know who that is? How many mares a pinche caballo mates with?"

"María, you remember her," JJ said.

"Oh yeah, seguro, cómo que no? Not that many Marías in the world. Or is she the transnational or transvestibule, whatever they say, that was always on the corner and liked only you so much."

JJ laughed. "She only liked every boy who passed on the street."

"Sorry you missed out," he said.

"María Sandoval," JJ told him. "That María."

"Our neighbor's María who you liked when she was in elementary school? Sweet innocent girl too young for you, our neighbor's daughter?"

"She was in middle school, and I was a senior in high school and hung out with her sister! And these days both of us are way out of college."

"That's some good news."

"You'd still like her, Dad," JJ said.

"Shouldn't she be married by now?"

"Dad, listen," JJ told him. "I talked to Tina."

"Good that you talk to your sister," he said. "Job's good? You didn't get fired? I can't loan you much if anything."

"I'm doing way good. You know that."

"Your sister isn't. I worry about what she's got going."

"She's worried about you," JJ said. "We're both worried about you."

He didn't say anything.

"Are you okay, Dad?"

"I'm not sure what you're asking me."

"She was telling me is all."

"Telling you what?"

"That you've been having a rough go of it," JJ said. "We know it's hard to be alone. Without mom, without me or Tina nearby. Back there, it's not the same. Nothing's the same. Things change. The neighborhood's getting rundown and old too."

"I'm not sure what Tinita means. She's got so many babies, all she'd need is to take care of an old man, too."

"That's what I'm talking about, getting old."

"A lot is still the same here. Just older than it was."

"Having old problems," JJ said. "It happens."

He didn't say anything.

"What I want to say is that you could come here," JJ said. "I'm buying a big place, and we'd love for you to live with us. I'm doing that good, dad. We're talking about getting married, too."

"What kind of old problems?"

"Come on, pops,"

"Name a thing."

"Okay then. Tina told me that lately you are like a madman looking around the house for some flashlight you say you bought that you didn't but you think you did and lost it."

That stopped him.

"Doesn't sound so great, does it?" JJ said. "Is it true? Are you going around like a crazy old fool looking for a flashlight?"

He had to stop. To think a few seconds.

"It's nothing, Dad. We all get old. Just better to not be alone if we can."

"A mini-mag light. Doesn't everybody go loco crazy looking for things they lost? Doesn't everybody lose things, go loco crazy until they find it?"

"Sure. But…"

"So what're you gonna say after I tell you I found it?"

"You found it," JJ said flatly, doubtful.

"Yes sir, I found it," he said. "In the mess of that room that was your bedroom a hundred years ago. I finally remembered I'd gone in there to change the lightbulb."

"Where was it?"

"In one of those stupid boxes too high for me. Why I never looked."

JJ didn't say anything.

"Tell your sister," he said sharply. Then he calmed himself. "I'll tell her. It is nice. That she worries."

"It's that we don't live close," JJ said.

"And nice what you said. Your offer."

"It's still there, Dad."

He didn't know how, or what, to say.

"It's good here," he told him. "It's not so bad getting old. It's not so bad. I remember back, so much here, and I'm still here, and the house still lives, too." He wished he could tell Junior about the foxes, that one fox, from the backyard to the driveway and across, but it wouldn't sound so good to him. Sometime, at a better time. "I'm doing okay, mijo," he said finally, fighting back embarrassing tears.

He bought another purple mini-mag flashlight first thing the next morning. He was absolutely certain the lost purple one was somewhere inside the house—he'd say he 'found' it until he really did—but quietly buying a new one was the solution. The idea just flew out of him when he woke up early in the morning, and it made him as happy as he was for the bright squawk and chirp of birds outside.

44

Prima

I was lucky to have my Tía Velma. My old man disappeared when I was too little to have even a fuzzy memory of him. He either went back to México and got stuck, or found a new mamita there, or here. Who knows? My mom—whether she shouldn't have been a mother, or was too young when, hard to pick which or what else—passed me off to my Aunt Velma, her sister. Often enough at first, until I lived there all the time. For me that was just how it was, and there was lots worse. There I had my Uncle José and my aunt, two primos and two primas, and it was all their lives and not just mine.

We were a family like in a TV show that was never on any TV. The room for that TV was called the TV room. It was made of half the garage, with the TV in the corner and two couches along two of the walls. For a while there was a raggedy chair, too, for Tío José, until they finally bought another TV set for their bedroom. We chamacos, and sometimes Tía and Tío, too, could all fit tight watching whatever if everybody cooperated. Once everybody else went to their rooms and beds, at night night, one of those couches was my bed. I slept with my head near the screen. Sometimes, lots of times but not always, I fell asleep with it on. Tía got me an old bookcase, its shelves my dresser. I lived simple, only a couple pairs of pants, a few T-shirts, two white always folded nice cotton ones for church, where I went when I was told to, and a few chones. Modest, I dressed in an empty space in a corner at the end of the couch. I never needed a bedroom. I remember that I felt happy about it all. Maybe it was more like relieved, but back then I'd say I was living real. I completely accepted being an abandoned puppy dog. I was a goo' boy. I wagged when I got treats, I cowered guiltily and hid on the couch when voices were loud.

I hadn't seen Aunt Velma in so many years, it was like another lifetime ago. And my primos had become figures from an ancient period: There was Joe Jr., the oldest, whose whole body was tatted cholo by 16, when I was settling there in their house and knew little what any of that was. He'd made it through juvie and out and then signed up for the army—didn't happen and I don't know why—until he got a long stint in the pinta, San Q, for armed robbery and attempted murder. He did worse than both. His little brother, my primo Alex, made good grades and ended up going to UCLA to study history. To me that sounded so close to heaven as it was far, far away from my couch life. He became a Brown Beret, which was way chingón. He was my four-star shiny hero, but in truth, I didn't really understand a lot he said when I got time with him. I thought it was because he was such a marijuano. I got stoned around him not even taking hits. My youngest prima, Crissy, she was younger than me. So young, around her I stood tall and suavecito and like a future badass. Except she was my prima, a baby girl, and, you know, her parents took care of me. Still, I felt crazy about her. I swore she flirted with me—it didn't matter if it wasn't true, believing was fantasy enough.

She was too *mush*, as a friend back then would say. When she had to be 16, I was working full-time and going to junior college full-time, living and paying on my own for my own self. One night I went to dinner at Tía Velma's. It'd been a few months since I'd been back. Crissy was gone. She'd met an Arab sheikh and they married, and she was gone, school days over. Aunt Velma told me Crissy was already living in the Middle East—where he was from, she told me in case I didn't get it. I thought it was funny, nuts, impossible, maybe even not good. My Aunt Velma said it was a lot of money, and Crissy was rich now, a princess! Crissy was, she said, already wearing gold and diamonds and rubies before they left from LAX. Uncle José nodded.

* * *

Aunt Velma called asking if she could spend the night. I didn't want to say yes. I did want to say no. But I couldn't do that, right? She'd never asked any favor before, ever. I owed her…a lot. She had left the house in LA—South Gate actually— after Uncle José had died. Aunt Velma moved to San Antonio, where Uncle José's elderly mom was. Velma took care of her. She lived in her house. She didn't have to tell me she thought it would become her house, but I knew she believed it. She didn't work, didn't do a wage job. She got Social Security from Uncle José's death. She had no other money. Now she told me she'd needed to go to LA and was on her way back from there, and she didn't want to pay for another motel room.

I was living in El Paso with my girlfriend, Emily. El Paso was where I was born and where my mom was from. I thought of it as the Chicano homeland, and I wanted to live there— though I can't explain why there and not like San Francisco or Mexico City, or, say, Peru near Machu Picchu. I thought I needed to be there is all. And I was extremely happy working for the *Herald Post*, even if it was almost no pay, covering high school sports but not UTEP basketball (yet). It was even better for Emily because she had a gig with a cross-cultural-international Mexico-USA institute. I never expected to meet anyone like her in El Chuco. She'd gone to Brown, way above me. We lived in a three-bedroom hacienda-style apartment on a hill that stared south and across the Rio Grande and to the dark horizon beyond Ciudad Juárez.

I told Aunt Velma yes. Reluctantly because she was with Mari, my other prima, who was my age. Not as princesa pretty as Crissy, not as smart as Alex, less trouble than Joe Jr., she had a little of each. She also had ridiculous boyfriends too early, and gave up a baby for adoption, and more. Young, she smoked mota always, drank too much, and gave glue a chance. She sobbed for long hours, and she had raging tantrums. She came home late, she slept late, she didn't like jobs, and they didn't keep her very long if one happened. She stole from people and stores and cars and got caught. She was arrested and convicted. She did a little juvie. Because she didn't watch TV much ever, she wasn't near my couch often, so we weren't very close. I thought she didn't really like me in her home, good dog or bad. I guess I didn't really like her back.

Emily was all for it. She was excited to meet one of the stars of my TV couch series, Tía Velma. And she didn't disappoint. Velma came with her whitening hair looking not wind but broom-swept, her Walmart dress like it was on backward, or something wrong, or like she'd slept a week on the streets. It probably seemed so much worse because Emily and her were hugging too long. It emphasized how perfect Emily was, contrasted unfairly. Casual, work, or formal, she looked like she was living in Paris, even in the subtlest waft of luxury fragrance. Aunt Velma had unmistakable BO. She did say how they'd been driving for over 12 hours, since five in the morning. And of course that meant she alone drove. Emily was the greatest. Appeared to notice nothing out of place, said all the best and sweetest things about Velma's beauty, youth, vigor, figure, and fortitude. She even admired Aunt Velma's sneakers. They were bright yellow and, Emily said, seemed much more comfortable than hers. Emily was wearing sandals that were dipped in gold, which allowed her always so lovely dark-cherry-painted toenails to show off her feet's flawless complexity. Aunt Velma was 100 percent flattered by the shoes compliment. They'd stayed near a Target, and they were even on sale, she explained proudly.

Mari had little—nothing—to say or show off. Not just to Emily, but to me. Walking a few steps behind her mom, it seemed more like a few rooms away.

On the phone call the day before, Velma, embarrassed, had to tell me why she was coming with my prima. That Mari had finished serving four months in the Orange County jail. Though she didn't get convicted for it, it was because she'd been accused of robbing some rich, powerful men. They were blaming her for it, and she didn't rob anything.

But, I asked, if she didn't get convicted of it, then why did she have to stay in jail?

They couldn't prove it was her, but they wanted to charge her with something.

What?

A lesser crime. And since she had previous arrests, it was a lot easier to make the charges.

Of what?

It was nothing to worry about, Velma assured me. What mattered was that she was released. Aunt Velma had to get her out and away from there though. Mari had to get out of LA and that state, start fresh in San Antonio and Texas.

But what was it for? I thought it probably did matter some.

Aunt Velma really didn't want to have to tell me, but she figured out that I wasn't going to stop asking. And she wanted to sleep over. It was costing her a lot more than she imagined. She told me it was solicitation.

It took me a few spins around my head to even ask what the hell that was. Wasn't that a man's crime?

She told me that that was what she meant. It wasn't true.

Solicitation?

Yes. She told me that Mari had been given a bad lawyer too. It was like her lawyer worked for them.

It took a few squints for my mind to see that the answer was no. Not solicitation. Maybe that was the category of the arrest and charge, but there was—roughly speaking—a man-side charge and a woman-side charge. She got the woman charge of saying yes for money, which did have a specific word that Tía Velma omitted.

* * *

In our apartment, Mari hung back from Tía Velma, Emily, and me. Ashamed? Nah. Maybe weirdly shy? More like out of place, out of her element. More like she'd been here too long already. Or like she'd been locked up behind a heavy metal door for months and lived in a cold, gray 6x8 cement box, convenient furnishings aside. More like she wasn't really standing where we were.

Emily tried to hug her hello, too, but Mari turned side-ways. She didn't seem to want to even look at me , though when she first followed Aunt Velma in, she'd raised her eye-brows, put her right hand up to her face level, and wiggled her fingers hi. I felt uncomfortable too. I didn't know what to say either. That was Emily's gift, to always talk friendly. I hadn't told her a lot about why Aunt Velma had gone to get Mari. In fact, I said nothing. I didn't think it was polite of me, one, and two, I didn't want to make Emily feel...not safe or judgmen-tal. Which I think was a good decision.

Emily was an enthusiastic host. Though early evening still, Aunt Velma, certainly hungry like always, was clearly very tired. Emily quickly decided that we'd pick up dinner—my job—from a taquería nearby on Mesa. Not go anywhere in other words, and after, Aunt Velma could go to sleep as early as she wanted and sleep as late as she wanted. Emily insisted that she and Mari consider spending two nights even. Then we could buy them a super nice dinner tomorrow night. We could have a late breakfast tomorrow morning. She really liked a hole-in-the-wall restaurant, also near, that she said wasn't re-ally much of one, more like a motel's little diner with a dozen Woolworths stools around its counter. Lucy's because that was the cook's name. It had the best Mexican breakfasts in the Southwest! And Velma could sleep in our guest bedroom. The two of them could share that bedroom. We had a comfort-able Japanese roll-out futon for the floor—no couch in the living room for either of them (a wink wink, haha jaja for me that she didn't believe, rightly, Aunt Velma would recognize). Aunt Velma was, of course, overwhelmed and enthralled. Encantada, Emily might say in her Mexico City–learned Spanish. Yes yes, Aunt Velma was starving. She wanted to go to sleep right then. She feared if she shut her eyes, she wouldn't wake up. She'd miss dinner and...wide awake at 2 or 3 a.m. and...she had diabetes 2, and she had to eat. So it was all set.

During the excited planning conversation between Emily and Tía Velma, Mari did speak to me about finding a bathroom. Leading her, I both noticed and didn't that she went in with a small suitcase. I only remembered that when Emily showed Aunt Velma to the bathroom and Mari was still inside, Emily led Aunt Velma to the other bathroom in our master bedroom. When Mari came out in the living room, with the suitcase, showered, she was wearing new jeans and a T-shirt as black as her wet hair. She had new shoes like her mom's, only black instead of yellow. Emily gushed about how hip and beautiful she looked. Very New York, she told her. Mari stared at her blank, or like a cat might, the eyes, so still, they seemed to be more listening than seeing. Though she was drying her hair with one of Emily's bath towels, Emily didn't flinch. I, for instance, wasn't even allowed to splash water near one. She pretended to not notice or care excellently.

Aunt Velma suggested she shower next. Emily said she'd go to her office—that was the third bedroom—and pull up the menu and call in an order. I said I'd drive out to get it. Mari, her hair less wet, was dead asleep, Emily's towel wrapped around her head.

* * *

We had a take-out feast: tacos de chuleta, pastor, bistec, champiñón, nopal. Frijoles charros, arroz, queso fundido, guacamole, cebollitas. Salsa de árbol y verde y pico de gallo. And four flanes de coco for dessert. And Emily plated it all for our dinner table like it was French, on silver platters. Aunt Velma opened her eyes as wide as her mouth. Mari stared the same as earlier.

One new minor problem: our roommate, Dylan Taylor slash Taylor Dylan, came back right then. He'd been Emily's idea since the beginning. We didn't need a roommate. We had plenty to pay for the apartment on our own. That is, she did at birth. Also, she made un chingo from her job. And it was her who disliked him the most. Me, I thought he of two first names was, mostly, a fucken spoiled culo. She, on the other hand, didn't like that wherever he momentarily nested, stopped moving, like a bird, he left droppings. Shoes and T-shirts were anywhere, just like Q-tips and nail cuttings or used Kleenex or hairs, from a comb or shaver, say. Wrappers and boxes and envelopes were not trash-worthy in his world. He never cleaned. Toilet, sink, or shower. Towels, for instance. Like the luxury towel that Mari used, which wasn't supposed to be there for him. There was no yours and his in the kitchen. Emily focused her irritation on two items there. Her Silk milk, for lunch smoothies, and her one fat-content treat, half-and-half. They were the straws that weighed on her back and rose her blood pressure. She wanted him out. I told her I'd tell him, but she'd say no, wait. For a while I suspected he was an old lover. He was handsome in a rich, slimy way that we who aren't can see. Perfectly mussed curls of hair, chic, high-end threads that could seem old and sloppy to an untrained, un-pedigreed eye, staged like a fashion ad. Emily did not care in the slightest if he had a woman spend a night now and then. He drove an older unwashed beamer. In tech, he could work anywhere, though sometimes he had to be in New York or the Bay Area for a week or two.

Whatever, he wasn't around very much. Two weeks at most a month. He thought El Paso was interesting. The border, Mexico. The quiet. He loved the apartment, he told Emily and me, and we were the only family he had to go to.

That night, with him there too, there wasn't enough over-abundance of food to Emily. In particular, the flan. I was fine without, but Emily, frustrated with any sudden imperfection, insisted that she be the one without. She really preferred watching her weight, inarguably ridiculous. Aunt Velma was heavy, and she swallowed hers whole and then ate Mari's too.

Once everyone was done with the meal, Emily offered Argentinian wine, Mexican beer, or French cognac. Beers went to Taylor Dylan and Mari, cognacs for Emily and me (like a good boyfriend), and for Tía Velma, another flan that I, way too full, had only a spoonful of.

Emily finally insisted the attention be on the other family houseguest, Mari. What had she been doing in Orange County? Did she live inland, or on the beach? They had such lovely beaches in Corona del Mar andNewport Beach.

I hadn't told her that Mari had been in jail in Orange County.

Aunt Velma was definitely not at ease.

Mari said she lived in a few places. For at least a month, it was with my mother. She looked at her mom after she said that.

Aunt Velma gave her the shut-up eye. Obviously, Mari wasn't supposed to say anything about anything that brought her here, but less than that about my mom, her aunt. I hadn't heard from my mom in so many years, I had no idea where she was and didn't ask. I really was okay with it. I got over that in my couch years. A decade-plus later at this point, I decided it'd be best if she, my wherever-she-was mom, were the one to ask about me when she was ready.

Mari went on, after a quiet pause, that she'd had a few lousy jobs. Emily laughed, saying how most were, weren't they? Laughing, though, in fact, she'd never had a bad job ever. She wondered if Mari really didn't like at least one there.

Maybe. But no.

What was the maybe?

She gave away cigarettes at clubs for a while. Gave them away?

She passed them out. They were a promotion. A new brand. People wanted a cigarette?

They were in a box.

And they paid well for that? Because you were…pretty, and sexy? Emily had emphasized that Mari was awfully pretty. She was too sexy, if anything, so that made sense.

They dressed the girls up in short, red frilly outfits with black see-through stockings.

That would certainly draw attention.

The outfit pushed the boobies up.

Aunt Velma told Mari to please not talk like that.

Emily asked if a job like that paid…well. Because it couldn't have been full-time.

No. Not without the tips.

Oh, so there were good tips?

Not always. Not usually. Drinks mostly. Sometimes the tips were really good though. One big tip was all it took. Old men trying to get some.

Aunt Velma stood up and said she thought that was enough. That she and Mari should get some sleep now. That they had to get up in the morning.

Emily now worried about what she thought had been a perfect plan. Now Aunt Velma and Mari weren't staying two nights? Aunt Velma was extremely tired and upset with Mari for talking so much, but she wasn't saying why. And where would they sleep if now Taylor Dylan, who was supposed to be gone at least 10 more days, was home and the guest bedroom was back to being his bedroom? But he offered his room up to both Aunt Velma and Mari. In other words, as Emily had it. He would take the couch.

But Mari said she wasn't sleepy because she had taken that nap before dinner. After Velma went to the guest room, while Emily and I cleaned up, Taylor Dylan asked if she wanted to go along with him to a place he liked here in El Paso. That maybe they could go over to Juárez if she'd never been. She didn't ask any questions, had no hesitations. She said sure. It was the first and only word she'd said to Taylor Dylan.

After they left, Emily said that, though she didn't speak up, she was a little unhappy because of Taylor Dylan leaving with Mari. I was a little worried about it because of Aunt Velma, but I'd said that to Mari before they left. Mari just shrugged. The dishwasher full, kitchen and dinner table cleared of any dinner clutter and clean enough for a photo, Emily went to her office.

I said I'd meet her in our bedroom later. I was thinking. Thinking how much Mari was like my mom in her wild strength. When I was so little, she was my mom taking care of me. My mom was always fun and laughing and playing with Mari. Mari loved to see men stopping and staring at my mom, how she ignored or gamed them, teased, overpowered them. Mari laughed so much back then. When I started living on the couch full-time, I didn't see Mari much. When I did, I'd ask her about my mom. She loved my mom so much I think she wouldn't say. After a while I stopped asking Mari anything. After a while she practically never looked at me when I did see her.

From the spacious deck with the huge view of the desert, where I was living my own life, looking at and beyond the border below to the edge of moving earth...I wanted the past to be the past.

* * *

It wasn't early, but it certainly wasn't late in the morning, and yet I was the first one up. I mean compared to Aunt Velma. Emily didn't count. She always got up early for her work, which was every day like me. She was in her office, door closed. I had a championship b-ball game to go to at two. Unusual was that Emily hadn't made coffee. Probably so she wouldn't wake up Taylor Dylan slash Dylan Taylor on the couch. He didn't usually sleep late either. I absolutely had to have coffee first thing, and so I was making it. I didn't care if it woke him up.

Dylan Taylor staggered near me. He hated the piercing noise too. I asked questions because he was standing too quietly.

He got in way late.

No, I told him I didn't hear.

Yeah, they had a good night. Yeah, they went to Juárez for a few hours. Hey, did I know she'd never been there or even here in El Paso before?

I didn't understand why that would surprise him.

Because he thought all of us were from here, crossed here, lived here a while. He laughed.

I actually thought he kind of believed it.

He said my cousin...He stopped and stared at me half-smiling, half-perplexed. The dictionary word that might suit was *sardonically*. A word a sports reporter never used.

The coffee was brewing.

I didn't know what he was getting at.

That she was strange.

I didn't have any comment for that.

He stepped a little away after I poured him his coffee. He was adding some of Emily's half-and-half from the fridge. Closing the door, he said she sure had a body, dude. And, here I quote, "You gotta hit it while it's hot."

Instead of just sitting at the dinner table where I had my laptop, my coffee mug next to it, furious, I popped Taylor Dylan in the chest with both of my open palms. He was totally unprepared and went crashing into a chair he'd pulled out for himself and even stumbled so that the antique table itself groaned and slid, everything on it falling off. When he regained control of himself, steadied his body, he swung with a right. Now I myself would have said he probably was the better athlete. He skied, he played racquetball, he had gym memberships, whereas though I did play b-ball and ran track for a few years, it wasn't for college scholarships. I was only good enough for high school teams. But like a pro boxer, I blocked his wild punch with my left arm, and my right hit him hard between his nose and eye. And I went to another left and right. He was backing against the table when he decided to come at me low, headfirst, like a bull with horns, to tackle me. Instead, he drove me back some. He came up looking bad. I pushed him, I hit him. Like a barroom brawl in a Western, he flew backward, and the table, like a movie prop, first lost a leg before it collapsed entirely with him on it.

We weren't done. We had been making a lot of noise, from us crashing into shit and breaking whatever was nearby to our voices going animal. Emily ran in screaming for us to stop it now! We could hear and see her some, but I was stepping over the wooden table leg for more, and he, bleeding from his mouth and nose, was trying to get up. I was yelling, crazed.

Emily pulled on my left arm as hard as she could. Aunt Velma came around to my front side to push me away from him. He stood up yelling back. Emily jumped in between us begging for Dylan Taylor to stop too. Both of us did stop. Emily was crying. I don't know what Velma was saying. Emily got Dylan a dishcloth to wipe away blood. I couldn't stop hearing my breath, not a word Aunt Velma was telling me as she kept talking, pushing me out of the dining area.

Soon there was a pounding at the door. EPPD. The two officers came in, the lead one talking, looking both ways at us, the one behind close to the open front door, his hand an inch above his holstered handgun. They wanted to know if anyone was hurt. Was Emily, still crying, injured? Was this a domestic dispute? Taylor Dylan started yelling yes, but Emily yelled no. They yelled back and forth at each other, Emily pleading to let it end, please let it end. Though she had no idea what or why it happened, she told the police officers no, it was only a dumb boys' fight. She was sorry. They said they would have to make out an incident report, and if either of us wanted to press charges, me or Dylan Taylor but mostly him because he was bleeding from his nose, we could in the next 30 days.

Ten minutes passed, or 20, who knows. Dylan Taylor was in the bathroom, and Emily was talking to him. Tía Velma was walking back and forth from him to me. I was sitting on the couch. I was fine. I was planning, any minute, to get up, go and clean and wipe away all the mess. Then Mari was standing between me and the hallway to the other rooms. She was looking right at me. She saw me sitting there, on this couch. I looked back at her, too, and she sat next to me on the couch and asked me if I was okay. It was like we would know each other forever.

The Dick, Casillas

I LIKE TO STOP AND SAY HI TO AYISHA WHEN I CHECK
in at the gym. She's usually there, though I'm there more. I
come six days a week, either 11 or 1:30. I used to get there
at 2 but there's a TV sports show I watch that comes on at
2, lasts an hour. If I want to watch that while I'm on a machine, I get another half hour of exercise without noticing it,
almost cheating, if you see what I'm saying. Minimum I want
is 60 minutes. I don't know how I or anyone used to do exercise before they had machines with cable TV. I'm not buying a thousand songs or a hundred CDs. I can't take the radio
stations anymore, the music there, impossible to find anything
that isn't old and heard and heard and heard. I feel like a perv
listening to some new top-40 station at my age—I do that on
the down low alone in my car. In the gym, TV on the machines wins.

Once in a while Ayisha and I chitchat. About nothing
always. Usually I just take a pause in my step and *hey hey,
whadaya say?,* tap the formica, and I pass on by. She and
I have disability in common is why the connection, nothing
much else, though that's also enough. I'm an older brother,
used to it, but she's too young to not be happy all the time. I

get more self-conscious when she's at the desk with Casillas. He's a little dick. So many tats all over his arms and legs and back and even up his chest and neck, his skin color is blue. He thinks he's badass. Accomplished somehow, skilled at whatever. I'm not *that* old. Can't happen. I don't for one second think he's someone I can't deal with. I don't like that he takes away from my big brotherly feelings for Ayisha. That's what he does though.

I can't do free weights now because I could hurt myself or someone else, so I go to the weight machines. I actually prefer them. They're better than they were back in the day. I have a few I like—quads, calves, abs, deltoids, traps, biceps, triceps, pecs—but I can't always do them all. Puts me down for the next day if I'm not careful. I pick two to four. I tell people, I've decided not to do the next Olympics, so I go easy.

I like to lift. Ever since I was a baby, that's the one that makes my body feel strong in the *ya no* weakness that comes with the last lift. I set the pin anywhere from 60 lb to 90 lb, depending on whether I want to do more per three sets, my usual, or just burst my buttons doing fewer with more.

There are a lot of older folks here at the gym. Could be because of the time of day. Many even older than me, by years, or even a decade or two. They're all impressive for being here in their routine. Women and men, pretty close to equal numbers. There's this one older guy who, whenever he sees me, stares into my eyes like he knows me, expecting me to...I don't know. Say hi? If he knows me, I'm not sure why he doesn't say so. It got so that I started thinking I knew him back, and he began to look familiar to me, too. Once, as I approached from a distance, I saw he was on the machine I liked most and usually went to first. I didn't change my stride—my cane-free limp, better said—and was moving on to another one, and I'd get it tomorrow. But as I got closer, that man stopped. He got up before I could pass by and then stared at me like he does, and I think offered a smile, or close, or it was just kindness. Like to a friend. He didn't say anything but I did. I said *Hey, real nice, thank you*, while he went off.

Not like he couldn't know me. Lots of older men know older sports. I had my days. I was good. Star linebacker, fullback, and I could even play safety until I either got too big or they got way faster by my senior high school year. I played baseball—third base or outfield, I could hit—and b-ball, though much as I liked it, I wasn't tall enough or quick enough—I couldn't be a guard—and too hot-headed. High school champion at Dominguez High, which was always terrible back in those days. We just about lost to any team, even the all-whiteboy ones. Except me. I'd win somehow in every story told. And I was a Mexican, so that never happened. I made news everywhere. National. I might've been the first Mexican ever. Or it was that I was taking attention away from all the Compton stars. Which was news. I was recruited across the country. Football and baseball. Local LA schools like UCLA and USC (though not enough there), and Stanford and Cal. Arizona, Washington, Nebraska, Notre Dame, Oklahoma. The teams I liked, that had baseball and football. I wasn't the smartest about colleges. I didn't know anyone who was. My parents didn't want me to leave town, even our neighborhood, because my dad was having health trouble and couldn't work, and my mom could barely speak English. It was a tough decision. Really hard. I knew nothing but football, baseball, and eating. I loved my mom's pollo en mole. I loved sirloin con una papa. I loved double cheeseburgers. I just took my high school coach's advice, the offer from Oklahoma. My mom, looking up at me because she was such a chaparra, was always about to cry, but my dad had come around. My brother and sister were proud. I'd be back. I'd make money. They thought I'd eventually drive back up in a *porcha*, which is a Porsche to non-Mexicans.

Make it quick: it wasn't even playing football, which I had just started doing there. Weeks. I was doing good, which is to say they liked me playing both sides of the ball still, and I liked it, and more newspapers were saying that too. National football news. I didn't get a lot of time reading much, but I saw and felt reporters, watching me mostly. I was in the hot gym, on the hot field, sweating, drinking and dousing water, eating a ton of anything that looked like food, and sleeping in what they told me was a dorm room but to me was just a bed. I had barely gone to classes, they were a blur, and I never did buy books. I didn't know what or where but, always hungry, of course I said hell yeah I wanted a giant steak, and the young assistant coach driving turned left in front of a pickup going maybe 50 on a sunny blue Oklahoma street and its front grill came through my door to where I was sitting with no seat belt on. I didn't die but I was a long time in the first hospital, and then came another and then another in a wheelchair, and then the wheelchair in no hospital. Like that. Years. It took a while to have no wheelchair. I might not walk too good, but I walk.

* * *

People pass by the recumbent bikes and the treadmills and ellipticals and step machines always. It's what you see when your eyes aren't on the TV. What I never see is Casillas's eyes on me. They happen to be looking away, seeing something else, someone else, anything else. They're busy, they're doing something, it's nothing personal, he's just hurrying by even when he's not really hurrying. It just happens that way, you know. Even when I'm off a machine, walking by, he can't see me while he's looking down, or *Gee, what just happened over there?* as he's getting close or passing me.

That older man seems to be at the gym at the same hours I am a lot, and he's at machines a few away and sometimes even right next to me. Casillas sees him all the time.

"Hey, Coach," he'll say. "You doin' good?"

I never really hear what the old guy says.

"You're lookin' good," Casillas says. "Good to see ya."

I just think Casillas is a dick. I don't see how anyone can blame me for this opinion. I don't know why he sucks up to this older man, but there's a reason and it's not a good one. He should at least call him 'sir.'

I'm not sure exactly what caused whatever it is about Casillas and me. It don't make a lot of sense to me. There's not a lot of us at this gym, and it'd seem like we'd have a connection in that way. Not that it's an expensive gym, exclusive. Not like Austin is racist or segregated. It does seem to be a very Anglo town, I'm not sure why. I live here with my sister and her generous husband Mike Loya—in a remodeled garage, like a one-bedroom apartment, near the river. He's a captain on the fire department and he's Mexican—from El Paso—and so are their kids, even though I wouldn't say any of them think about it a lot, or that their neighborhood is or ever was Mexican like where we grew up in LA or where Mike grew up in El Paso. That's kind of good, right? In fact here in Austin they like things Mexican. Besides cops and firemen—at least one Mexican woman there too, I met her—they like blankets and dinnerware and the food and the decor, and going to Mexico on trips and even Spanish as a language. The gym just isn't very much Mexican, and it seems like me and Casillas and every once in a while an older lady on her cell while she's on the bike—no talking on the phone in the gym is the rule—gossiping with a sister who's in Monterrey. Equally irritating if she were chattering in English.

My best guess is that it began at the desk. I was talking to Ayisha and we got to laughing. It couldn't have been about a lot or a little. I've strained to remember this whole time because it's all I could come up with and, really, it couldn't have been much. I'm old and she's not. I was talking to her because of her trouble, not to make any. Nothing else in my head, and it wouldn't have occurred to me that anything could bounce back. But I do remember that Casillas was on the other side of the desk too. Ahead of us at the laser reader, checking people in. And though I wasn't paying much attention, my memory's wide angle recorded more. He was frowning, pissed off. I assumed it had nothing to do with anybody but himself. We all can get like that. He said he needed her to be doing this, what he was doing, not him. She and I hadn't been talking that long I don't think, but it was long enough for a problem. I mean, we did start laughing like we were outside on a nice weekend day. She was at work. I wasn't. Nothing but time. She jerked herself out of relaxed mode when he said what he did. He scowled going away as she took his stool. I just figured it was about being at work. She blipped me in, and I went on through.

It was after that came his attitude. Seemed to grow by the day. That badass man strut got wider when he saw me. Like those tats were muscles. Walking by me like I was almost nothing, and that don't work with me. I know I'm not what I was, what I could've been. I know most don't know about that. A few do. They can still see it in a broken me. People who remember, remember me. Ones who know sports and sports stories. Who aren't dumb culos like Casillas who don't know shit. Who thinks the world is *only* what he thinks and knows about. That he's some kind of mero chingón at a gym where he's a personal trainer or whatever? Who sees me and goes, there's some old crippled nothing. But I can still take this punk how I am right now.

I did weight machines and I'm on a recumbent bike, the TV on. I'll go to my 60 mins and maybe I'll do more if I'm not sick of sitting here, pedaling. I don't know why I still like all this so much, but I do. I've loved gyms since I was young and they were always good to me. The old man who knows me, who I think I maybe know back, is a few bikes over. People are coming and going by in front of us and one is Ayisha. I don't see her in this area much. She has trouble walking the way she wants, and she's showing it today. She smiles at me as she comes and I say *Hey there, young woman!* and I'm smiling big, happy for both of us. She stops by me. It's partly for me, and I pretend it's only that, but I know it's not. She's hurting, a bad body day. She needs to walk more maybe, or maybe just not any more today. Some days aren't as good as others.

I offer her my seat. I say it's the comfortable one, making a face to say it's not at all. She laughs. She asks me what I'm watching. I'm about to play with that subject when suddenly Casillas is on the other side of my bike.

"They're waiting on you," he tells her. "You forgot?"

"She'll just be a minute or two more, big man," I say. "You need to give her a little more room." I'm not saying so, but mostly I'm talking about the joints in her hips that I know are bothering her.

"You don't need to worry about that."

He didn't actually say that to me though, because the words weren't said to my face, with his eyes looking at me.

"I think you shouldn't talk to me that way," I said.

Ayisha mumbled or so it seemed. I wasn't hearing her well. I was getting off my reclining bike.

"It's all right, Coach," Casillas said to the old man near me. "Please don't worry yourself."

I stood near him. He acted like he wasn't worried. Seemed like I was a foot taller, at least 50 pounds bulkier. "Is something bothering you that we should deal with here, now?" I asked.

"Coach," he said, waving his hand, looking at him because the old guy was coming over to us. He was ignoring me.

"Did you hear what I just said?" I said.

I might have stepped closer. Because then Casillas shoved me away. I'm not sure why I didn't expect that, why it caught me so off guard, but it did. And I do have my own wobbly leg issues. I'm not the most stable two-legged gym rat. I stumbled. I'm not sure what it was exactly, but I think my foot caught the bike's pedal and I went backwards. I went down hard because of the foot tangle. On the ground I knew I couldn't pop back up if I tried, I could tell. Always hard for this body to get off the ground, even when it isn't hurt. My head hit another machine and there was a cut on the side of my forehead. My back didn't like what it hit, or how, either.

People gathered around and worried about the cut on my head. I wouldn't say anything about my twisted foot. I

68

couldn't get up easy because of it. It was all still there, not broken in my opinion, but it was going to hurt.

Seemed like I was stuck on the ground.

"Do you need help?" the old man asked me. He was the first there, squatting down to me. "Can you stand?"

"Should we call an ambulance?" someone asked. "What do you think, Coach?"

"I can't believe that happened," I tell the old guy. "I completely lost my stupid balance and then I lost it all." I wanted him and everyone listening to understand.

"You need help?" he asks again.

"My pride," I tell him privately. He did look awfully familiar.

"You gotta let that go so you can see what's really hurting," he says.

I laugh. "That sounds like some advice I should take."

* * *

I was out for a few weeks. I wore the boot with the velcro straps to the gym that first day back to make sure I didn't re-injure that ankle. I felt happy going back. I always felt like the gym made me feel better about everything. It was my one sure thing. I say that's how it was for that old guy. I decided I wanted to meet him. Introduce myself to him and thank him for that day they took me to the hospital. He had my back.

Ayisha wasn't at the desk. I was hoping she'd be happy to see me. Casillas wasn't there either. Maybe he'd be unhappy to see me, maybe he'd want to smile. I had to force myself to not think about him. I walked straight to the bikes because I wanted to move my legs. I was even slower walking with the boot.

The lady next to me said hi and asked if the foot was all that still remained. She was here then, she told me. I recognized her, but it was the first time we'd talked.

"As dangerous as ever," I said.

"It looked worse," she told me.

"Stupid fall," I said

"The coach told me about you," she said.

"About me?"

"From football," she said.

"I don't know him," I admitted, "but I want to now. He's a football coach here in Austin?"

She laughed. "You don't know Coach Royal?"

"No ma'am."

"I assumed you'd played for him... The Longhorns' football stadium is named after him, for goodness sake. You don't know Texas's greatest coach?"

"I've only lived in Austin a little over a year," I said.

She didn't even hear me say that. "You don't know the news, either, do you?"

I didn't have to say no.

"He passed."

"Just since... I haven't been here?"

She nodded pedaling, and I pedaled too.

"That's sad," I told her. "I'm very sorry."

She nodded. "He had a good life. We all loved him."

I asked my cuñado about him, I asked my sister. They laughed at me. Of course they didn't know him personally, like me, but even they knew who he was by the stadium name and the news and Texas football everything all the time. We'd even been to two games together there. That is, I myself had been to Darrell K Royal stadium both those two times.

I couldn't get it off my mind that I missed the chance to talk to him. That I didn't know who he was, but he knew who I was, back when, that maybe he even wanted to know me the way I was now. It dizzied me. Seemed worse than dumb.

Back at the gym I learned from Ayisha that Casillas had been let go because of the incident. She could barely tell me without tears. She liked him, of course meaning more than that. I'd missed that, too. So if I saw her behind the desk I only waved when I blipped in now—she didn't work that spot ever now. I was back in my routine, a little slower at the beginning until my foot seemed all good again. The weight machines first, a couple to a few, then to aerobics, an hour, where I watched a sports talk show. It wasn't very much. I knew it. It didn't matter. That was what I had left, what I wanted again.

I love the gym. It's where I go. It was me before my football and baseball life. When I was stronger, bigger. Like I'm not now. The world really is more than dicks like Casillas. Who, like me, will miss too much that is right next to him. Some love the outdoors. I love to hear the loud silence of the gym. The plates of weight machines smacking down, the groans from pushing hard, whirs of ellipticals, bikes, fans. Once I was going to be a star, or even was a star, and now I'm here alone, working out with what I still got, and nobody knows me, or sees me, and that's right where I began, and it was good then, like now.

Answer

I WAS HERE BECAUSE I WANTED TO BE. I DIDN'T HATE
school, I especially didn't hate learning. The main thing they
taught me, yelling into my face, was that I was wasting their
time and money. It did take me a few incidents, and some
growing years, to allow the words of these wise teachers to
work for me: Wasting *their* time and money? So I got done
with their troubles and their finger-pointing. At the part-time
job I already had—my uncle Jorge (pronounced in easy Anglo,
George) ran an industrial laundry he called the plant—and I
asked him if I could go full-time. He didn't have any question,
didn't blink. He said he'd started working before they'd invented school. To him and lots of people I came up around, I
was grown, young only en este lado, on their side.

Forty-eight hours a week, 7 to 3:30, and I was making coin.
I bought me a nothing-special, four-door Ford—no more bus!
I was shifted into the clean area, the unpressed washed sheets
and unfolded towels, and that was better too. I loved getting
morning café with lots of sugar from Rosa, who'd been working there over 30 years, the same as my uncle, who knew my
mom. She gave some to me every day if I got there before 6:50,
because at 6:51 she put her thermos away. Herminio, an older

73

man who was from a Mixtec village with a name I could never pronounce, had extra tacos warmed (rolled like burritos) for me at the first whistle break—frijoles with onion and tomate, con chilecito. Life was good like this, and I got paid. The guys I worked with, Juanito and Gerónimo, they were older, sharper, and I liked being around them and learning the work and everything else. Juanito, who would say he was from El Paso, but really Juárez, though really really San Luis Potosí, was the oldest of us, the longest at the job, which was almost five years. He was either 24 or 27, depending on the day you asked. Gerónimo was 21 and had spent time in prison. He said he was a Mexican Indian from Arizona. Since he didn't speak English or seem to know any Native language either, I didn't believe he was telling the whole truth, but I didn't question him. His face was an Olvera Street wood carving of an Aztec, so harsh and rough it could've been gouged by a machete. Me, I was born at the Texas–New Mexico border but raised in LA and I was hungry to learn, there was so much I didn't know in the real world. Even though I had lived most of my life in this big noisy city, I was more del campo, like an innocent country boy. The two of them told me lots. They told me dicho-like truths about cabrones and pendejos, and they especially liked to be expert about people who worked in the plant.

"Her," Juanito whispered when Faby walked by, his eyes down as if in prayer. She was pretty and swayed. "She'd be good for 10 babies."

We laughed. He meant she was a chichona, big in the boobies area.

"Brother," Gerónimo told him like he was talking to an alcoholic, "you forgot the four legal ones? You want a little illegal one too, you stupid?"

Four children was true. I didn't know a man could have so many so young.

"That one," Gerónimo told me of Jacinta, the one with curves who moved like she thought it was crazy for her to be working here. "She goes with the boss." He eyed me to catch if I showed anything. I gave up nothing. "Your uncle," he said, as if I didn't know or hear what he was saying.

"She's something," I told them both.

Really my uncle was the one who was something. Or that was how my mom saw him. My mom said he made my aunt pray more faithfully. My mom said it was men like him who made her go to prayers less. Of course that was about my father, who I can't say I ever knew any better than by a wallet-size photo I once saw. He was always back there in El Paso to me. Probably the kind of El Paso that Juanito had lived in once upon a time, if he ever really did. It did sound a lot better to me, even as I grew up, that she'd left him behind. When I was little, I thought of him as a vaquero, or even American cowboy, either one. He was riding hard, moving on so fast the rising dust seemed to be blowing the other way.

Neither guy said much about Isela. That was because they honored her. She was sweet, quiet, calm as 5 a.m., and she was married—which was never the end with any other woman, except with her it was. Even Gerónimo might have sighed like Juanito if he knew how to make any soft noises. She was an ideal. Her husband was from Chihuahua, which meant something powerful to both of them.

To me she was small, super cute, and in a way farther away category of life than me: in her 20s, a grown woman, a wild unknown. I was dumb and clumsy, my feet faster than my brain. Anyone would say Isela was shy. But once, when the beams of our eyes connected, it got so bright it could only be stopped by a forced looking away. Like magnets pulling, it was hard for me to not turn toward her. The first time I really met her up close was a morning I came to the lunchroom at 6:31, early early—I knew exactly because I punched the time clock—and I went right over to Rosa for morning cafecito. How could I have known that Isela would be sitting right next to her? Never heard of her being there, never was when I went before, even if it was usually 6:45. I'd never come in so early, but this day I did. Like I just had to. I didn't say a word, she didn't say one either, and yet I met her and she met me and we met.

Around then Hermi gave me a couple of tacos at break like always, and I went to go eat them in the lunchroom. I didn't ever go there for breaks or lunch. I fought to keep myself from staring over. She was with the women she worked with, not chatting like they were. She wasn't looking back at me either, but her not chatting or looking, to me, came out the same. After, I swore I could even tug at the pull of her eyes when she was working over there, even when she couldn't see me if she tried. That's how crazy I got. It was an illness.

Sometimes the three of us guys would be sorting through wet sheets to lay out for pressing in the mangle, and though I could see and hear Gerónimo or Juanito talking, it was like I was in another room, their mouths moving far away from where I was.

"¡Despiértate, vato!" Gerónimo's voice was like a slap.

Juanito was nicer. "Up up little babies don shoe cry..." He knew the rest even less.

I didn't say anything. I lied that I'd met someone. I was thinking Isela but I didn't say it. I exaggerated what happened, which was nothing but in my head, what I dreamed, played down that it meant much to me. Then I said she was kind of like her, like Isela.

"You are a baby," said Gerónimo. "Better you break your uncle's cookie jar."

"You don't want to go there," Juanito said. "You can't get married so young."

Gerónimo laughed at him cynically. "Don't make a baby. Make sure she's not already married."

* * *

I didn't go to church anymore, hadn't once since I was maybe 10, but I'd say I was like kneeling in a chapel, eyes closed, or focused on her, praying. Prayer all day, concentrating hard, only her, getting myself closer, purer in thought. I was dazed. Yet in another part of my mind I knew it couldn't be like praying at an altar, because, since she wasn't a saint but a real girl, a grown woman, Isela, who was years older than me, who was married, this could only be lust. It wasn't and couldn't be what I should want, should pray for, what God would grant me. My mom once told me she still believed in God (and the Santa Misa, even though she stopped going to church) but she'd quit praying as soon as she could. Her sister, my bad uncle Jorge's wife, told her that that was why she'd lost her husband, my father. My mom rolled her eyes and said my aunt lived in a sad fantasy world because no God would want her married to my faithless uncle. All this just got me more confused.

It was Herminio who rushed over to me while I was pushing an empty laundry cart to where we left empties. He'd never come over to me unless he had tacos to give me. He'd be happy, like I was an old person and he was the young one doing a good deed. This time, late in the afternoon, not smiling, secretive, whispery like he had to get to me alone, he wanted only me to know: la señorita needed a ride. He almost scared me with the news. First of all, how did he know about her and whatever she was inside my head? I hadn't told even Juanito or Gerónimo. It also came to me right then that I didn't really know why Hermi gave me tacos every morning break either. I only stared at him speechless. Not one word to say to him. And as quickly and suddenly as he came, he turned away and went back.

I didn't tell either Juanito or Gerónimo about this, either. I didn't ask them nothing about what to do or what not. My head was down for the last hours of the day. When I'd look up at them, I didn't too long because I didn't want to get any questions, laughter, mocking, sarcasm, wiseass advice, a stupid song, snicker, any hilarious joke. Once or twice I knew their looks between each other were about me. I wanted it all to be so nothing to me, to care so little, I wouldn't see them, I wouldn't hear them.

After the whistle, I was eyes open in my car, happy to be going. I didn't even like my car anymore or the money I owed my uncle—it'd been his—to buy it. Ashamed that I could be like this, I was half wanting it to stop. I thought that maybe I wouldn't come in tomorrow. I could call in sick. Maybe not come back at all. Another job. All these kind of thoughts popped up as I pulled away heading to my big brother's, the carpintero, except not a good idea because sometimes he'd have been drinking all day and, high once he got home, he didn't care about anything. Or maybe to my big sister's, except she'd be running after all her kids and her boyfriend's kids and ones she babysat for money. And I didn't want my compas to know all things with me out of school weren't all better than whatever they did, so not them. My older older sister maybe, but she was so perfect she was like a priest, even if she was female, and anyway I didn't want to confess love or lust or hear about me from her either.

Then I saw Isela walking on the sidewalk. By herself. My heart hit the brakes. I slowed, but I couldn't stop because of the traffic pushing me to move steady. I pulled into a red zone, near a fire hydrant, ahead of her. She wouldn't know it was me so I slid half over and leaned in the rest of the way, buzzed the passenger's window down and called out her name. I said her name like we were great pals, knew each other for years. We'd never talked one word. I probably was supposed to pretend I didn't know her name. She may not have known mine.

I got myself back to my side of the car, swung open the door, and stood, looking over the top.

She stopped and didn't move. She stared at me, barely looking. Then, "Oh, hi."

A car blasted its horn at me.

"I hope I didn't scare you," I told her.

Another car wove wide around, a couple of jerks called me names.

"I saw you walking."

"Yes," she said. She looked at me for a second.

I couldn't breathe right. "I was thinking. A ride. To home. Or where you're going, where you need." I wanted to sound OK. "If you want."

She came to my car and opened the door and she sat inside, in the front seat. "Thank you," she said. She didn't look at me at all.

I could barely think of what to say. And she seemed stuck, too. She apologized and thanked me too much, too quietly, directing me as I squeezed back into traffic. Our talking was a lot like the driving. I could barely pay any attention to where I was going, where I was, only the straight aheads, the lefts, the rights. That she was sitting there, that itself was beyond my mind's ability for much else. Then we were there.

"Wait, no," she said suddenly. "Not here. Farther, more ahead."

I rolled forward. "More...more still." Finally she said this was fine, told me to stop.

"You're OK here?" I asked.

She was smiling. "Yes, yes! Thank you!"

I got to look at her. For uninterrupted seconds. I could have swooned. I couldn't believe I could have ever met this girl, this woman... "If you need a ride tomorrow," I said.

She looked at me for more than one second, because she was happy, then nodded. "After work?"

"Sure!"

"You can?"

"At your service," I said in that bowing, humble Spanish expression.

"I have to go now," she said.

"Until tomorrow," I told her.

Nothing looked the same. I was so dumb, I didn't know I'd been living in paradise! I turned up my music , wishing I could throw louder gritos of love, cry the weakest of masculinity, and the fiercest. I drove, air beneath me.

* * *

I got to work the next day way early, about the same time as Rosa with her café, and angled myself to watch Isela punch in. She wouldn't look at me until once, a moment smaller than a second that flooded my eyes like a camera flash, and then she put a finger to her lips, her eyes down, so sweet with me in them, to tell me to shut up, to say absolutely nothing, to let nobody hear or see nothing. I understood!

I loved my job again. I loved my car again. I loved for the first time.

"What's going on with you, vatito?" Gerónimo asked me sarcastically. "Yesterday you were fucked up like a tecato with the shakes."

"What do you mean, little dude?" I said. He was older, more dangerous, and looked a lot of things more than the other older guys there, but he wasn't taller.

Juanito, who was as tall as a tall white guy, laughed. "Somebody took a nap."

"Maybe he got a raise from his uncle," Gerónimo said.

He was always saying I made more than they did. I didn't think it was true, but I didn't want to risk finding out by comparing checks.

"You get a raise?" he asked.

"He's probably happy because he bought a puppy," Juanito said.

Jacinta swayed to the bathroom.

"Kiddy kiddy," Gerónimo said quietly, meaning *kitty*. "You get a raise, too?" he asked me.

"I do wonder if he pays her more," Juanito said about Jacinta.

Gerónimo could never be lightweight. "You ever see her?" he asked me. "Like him and her not here at work?"

I shook my head and decided to go get another full cart to bring over to us. Herminio met me, excitedly it seemed to me, asking if I was all right. I said I was, as regularly as I could, not wanting to give anything away. That seemed to make him too satisfied. He told me he had tacos for me. He always did, so why did he have to say that? I thanked him and wished I meant it more, but it was too strange. It didn't matter, though, quickly forgotten.

What mattered was the end-of-the-day whistle blew and I got to go to my car. I saw Isela come out, and I knew she saw me too. She wouldn't look, but I'd say she was walking faster. I understood. Better that nobody knew. What I didn't know was how long to wait before I left for her, and it was hard for me to sit still. I couldn't wait too long, I was sure, but I didn't want to miss her either.

I think I came across her sooner than last, and this time I honked. Two little taps, beeps as short and cute as I could make them. She still jumped some and seemed to look around before she came to the passenger's door and scooted inside. I pulled away from the curb and into the mess of traffic.

"I'm sorry," she said so quietly. "I don't want people...anyone at work..."

"I agree, really."

"It's the gossip," she said.

"Of course, I understand the worry. We could pick a place. Farther up? If you want. And wait for me there, better?"

She chewed her lip.

"Same thing if you'd want me to get you in the morning..."

"No no," she interrupted.

"...so you don't have the long walk."

"No," she said again. "This is nice, very kind by itself."
Then she looked over at me.

My God, like I'd never seen a woman before. One who
smiled in my own car!

"Thank you. I'm so happy that you aren't bothered."

"Bothered? Impossible. I'm happy!" So happy I blurted out
this: "You're so beautiful!"

I'm not sure if she blushed—she was a morena, so who'd
know?—but, her face downward, she smiled like I'd never
glimpsed. "Thank you," she told me.

I felt stupid, a teenager. "I'm sorry," I said. "I shouldn't
have said that."

She shook her head certainly.

"I don't want you to think...," I went on, not sure how
to say that she was a grown woman, a married woman, and
I was...that I just quit high school. The real. I said, "I don't
mean to be disrespectful."

"No," she said, eyes on me. It was as if she'd moved closer.
I swore I could see stains of green in their brown. "It was very
nice of you."

I loved that there was traffic and we had to move so slow.
Also I didn't try to avoid any stupid driving in front of me. I
didn't remember a single turn or stop. How long it took me
to get to her place. Where I was, where I was going. I'd already forgotten the other facts. Reality. And I didn't think
she minded. Before she got out of the car, she hesitated. She
looked over at me. It was the longest time yet. I thought she
might reach and touch my hand. She didn't. That didn't matter either. I couldn't have taken that too.

And so it was for days that floated like months. Hidden.
Nobody knew. I didn't stare at her with longing sickness or

prayers. I worshipped her. It was real or fantasy, and I didn't care which, because...say I were to die. My life felt full.

Hermi was bringing me three tacos instead of the usual two. Why? He winked, the kind that was between us. He said, "You are young, I'm old. I've eaten plenty. Especially in the morning. I need less. So now you have one more. You need it." He winked, or it was something like one. I didn't really understand, but tacos weren't so much.

Gerónimo kept digging for things. "So what's going on, vato? You been acting all over the place. You get a bigger raise?"

I told him I wished he'd quit saying that shit. I didn't make any more or less than him.

"How much?" he asked.

I looked at him and shook my head. I was about to say when Jacinta popped into sight and he got distracted.

"That is a rich and tasty chicken," he said, watching her walk as long as he could, until the bathroom door behind her closed. He took more time after. "What do you think of her, vatito? You like?"

I didn't like this subject either.

"Or you can't let yourself because she's your Tía Sancha?"

What was I supposed to say? What could I possibly say?

* * *

Isela said I should come in.

"Where you live? Your casita?"

She'd touched me politely a few times by then, but this time it was like my whole hand by her whole hand. Really different. Her place was in the back, behind a bigger home. You had to get to it going around trellises of flowers—and then

84

came the cornstalks. The people in the bigger house grew corn in their backyard. I'd never seen that before—never been so close to real corn. Mostly cans, on shelves. If you didn't already know it was there, you'd never see the little casita at all. The door we came through was more for a shed, plywood so thin it didn't seem wooden, and instead of a doorknob was a cabinet handle, above it a latch and hook for a padlock that kept the door closed.

It took me a few breaths to figure out that the ceiling was lower than normal. I wasn't as tall as I felt. Things were nice enough from the floor up. A saggy sofa with a matching stuffed chair. A picture of Jesus, the one everyone owned, a couple of decorated crosses and a plain one surrounding it, a mirror in a gold frame. A narrow stove and short refri. The table was wrought iron, an outdoor kind. Above it was an old photo of Pancho Villa, a famous one with straps of bullets crisscrossing his chest. Three plastic lilies in a vase.

"Do you want a beer?" she asked me.

She didn't look as small. It couldn't just be the room's shorter height. There was so much more of her here. Bigger than her life at work. Than my life anywhere. Than me. I was so excited and I was terrified: we never once talked about the obvious subject.

"Or a soda if that's better? I'm having a soda."

"Soda. No, beer."

She brought me a can. "You hungry? A quesadilla?"

"No, nothing, thank you. You don't have to cook…"

I was on the couch when she sat. Close to me. She almost got my mind off the collection of ceramic gallos and the metal horses on a table sharing the space with an old lamp making a yellow light.

"So," I said finally, "your husband..." I didn't know why I said this. It was the last thing I wanted to talk about.

"You don't worry," she said. "Please?"

She was so close to me, my mind spun, either less or more, I couldn't say. I definitely didn't want to know her husband's name.

"I'm so happy when I am with you," she told me. "Are you happy?"

Happy wasn't it with me. When she kissed me, I began circling earth. Nothing about Isela—her lips, hair, cheeks, neck, back, waist—was like anything I'd ever touched before. When I took in normal air, I landed and my legs were running. I wanted out that paper door before it opened in at me.

At work the next morning, Isela didn't hide looking at me when she punched in. I was the one who looked down and away quick. I felt her watching everywhere outside me. Inside me I told her to stop it, or to be careful, to not let anyone know. Nobody knows anything, we hadn't done anything, my voice said, in no words, to her eyes, not staring, watching me. When I looked around, really, nobody was seeing anything, especially coming from Isela.

"Are you talking to yourself?" Juanito asked me.

I wasn't sure.

Gerónimo said, "Your girl tell you she's pregnant?"

"What?" I screamed, or just about. Way too loud for sure. I overreacted. I thought he knew about Isela and me, that they both did, and the rest. Which wasn't possible.

They both laughed. I don't know what sound came out of me.

"Vato," Gerónimo said, "calm yourself down." He cracked a smile. I had never seen a smile in his carved face.

"Even if your girl just told you she's having a baby, you're in good shape if you calm yourself," he told me. "Almost always a lie."

I didn't know which was stranger—him smiling or him offering real advice, dumb or not.

"Just don't go crying like a girl, vato."

He was back to his normal anyway, and at least his distraction settled me.

"Seems like you guys are on me a lot," I said.

Gerónimo kind of stopped everything and, nodding, did a whole check-me-out thing.

"No, it's nothing bad," Juanito said. "We're just seeing you."

"Seeing me?"

"We got no uncle here," Gerónimo said.

It took me a few seconds to realize that he said that to Juanito.

At break I was afraid Isela would come over to me upset, and there'd be nothing but eyes on us and gossip. So I headed where most went, outside to a lunch truck. Hermi chased me down. "You forgot these, mijo." Three tacos. He stopped, he breathed harder, but not from being out of breath. His voice kind of trembled. I swore all this was about Isela and it made me worry more. Before he left, I told him to wait a moment. And I almost asked him. I said thank you instead.

I fought hard against picking her up after work, forcing myself to walk away slow. That I shouldn't. I didn't get into my car too fast. I stalled many extra seconds waiting to turn on the engine. I used the brakes. I almost decided I would take another route.

I didn't tap my horn. No party-time blast, no cute beep-beep, just silence way ahead of her where I could pull over in a no-parking space. She rushed to the car, almost tripping a skinny old man walking with a fat dog, and when she got in, she started sobbing.

"I'm sorry," I said. "Everything's fine. Everything will be fine."

She didn't stop.

"Please, Isela," I told her.

She wouldn't say a word.

I couldn't talk either, so I took off and I got to her drop-off area. I didn't know what to do. I decided to stop close to her casita.

She looked up, her eyes on me through a waterfall. "¿Ya no me quieres?"

"Only too much," I said.

She slid over to me and soaked me in tears, crying and kissing. I parked the car not so close. She moved fast, but I kept up with her easy. I thought we would slow to that couch, but no, we went through a curtain where it was nothing but a closet of a room, empty walls and all bed that was a mattress, sheet, pillows, and a blanket, a ceiling so close it made us seem bigger than whatever was up in the sky on its other side.

"It's OK," she kept whispering. "All is fine, don't worry." She was the voice of heaven. "It's us. I love you, I want all of you."

I couldn't see anything but her, and it wasn't just the tiny room. I didn't feel anything but her. I didn't know anyone but her. It didn't matter where we were, didn't matter where I was going. If there was an answer from God, if I was in paradise or hell, if there was a should or a shouldn't, if it was sickness to hear *love* and float like a bubble of tingling starlight.

* * *

For who knows how many days or weeks I moved like everything was as it had been and always would be. When I got my sugary morning cafecito from Rosa, even though I saw Isela's eyes stuck on me clocking in, I didn't get stuck back. I was numb. I was in heaven or I was in hell. I didn't go toward the break room to see her, or run to the lunch truck at break to hide my eyes, my thoughts. I didn't want to get stupid about us. We were a perfect secret. When Hermi brought me tacos, I took them for granted. He was always so pleased to bring them to me. They were good for me, he told me, holding the foil wrap of them, just right, and I would really love them if I were as hungry as he was. I said he should keep them if he was hungry. He shook his head hard. Once I was, he said. These were for me, that's what he wanted. I needed them, he said. I laughed because they were tacos and it didn't make any sense, and he laughed with me too because I laughed. My uncle, he told me, liked them too. My uncle? Twenty-five years ago, when he first came to work here. My uncle was my age then, while he was old even then. We both laughed again.

After break, in front of a bin of just-washed sheets, I was trying to talk about Isela without saying it was about her. Sometimes I made as much sense as a drunk, and not even I could understand me. It was the secrecy, our bodies. That she was married.

"What're you talking about?" Juanito asked.

"That he's your wife's Sancho," Gerónimo told him.

"That's so funny," Juanito said. "You're like TV."

89

"You better check the color of the eyes in the next chamaquito who pops out," Gerónimo said.

"What're you talking about?" Juanito asked me again.

"Nothing, I guess," I said. Then, "Just how you know what's love."

Gerónimo laughed. It was a gut laugh, surprised him like a pointy-toed boot hit him right there. He never laughed.

Juanito took me serious, like we weren't in an industrial laundry sweating in 100 percent humidity and maybe the same in heat, giant fans swirling air like an outdoor wind and we were really on top of a mountain. He was gathering words for an answer when Gerónimo, his carved Aztec face back to usual, beat him to it.

"A knife too sharp to feel until it does," he said. "Lots of blood."

"That's hate," Juanito told him.

"También," said Gerónimo.

We all saw my uncle talking to Isela in the corner they worked. Jacinta was with her. She and my uncle walked her to the office.

I went for another full cart, taking the empty first.

Hermi said she was sick and wanted to go home early. He said, in that to-me-only voice, that it was her husband. Something, he said, always something.

I decided to go for more, to ask what if she were messing around. They knew nothing of me and her, suspected nothing. Nobody did.

Gerónimo made two fists and pulled them toward his hips a few times.

"Isela?" I said.

"I thought you were talking your tío's cookie baby," Gerónimo said.

Juanito shook his head. "Easier to get free rent."

"Her old man's old country," Gerónimo said. "He'd kill her."

"Not him?"

"Both."

"I'd stop breathing and die," said Juanito. "Not her."

"It's morning," Gerónimo said, seeing her leave the plant. "Probably that kind of sick."

"Lots of ways to be sick," Juanito said, "but a good bet if she were my wife."

She came in the next day, and I picked her up walking after work and we went into her casita. We didn't talk a lot ever, only what said we were happy when we were together. Besides, I knew so little. I didn't even know what I thought I knew very well. We went to the bed and we were like the only two in a world that nobody else had discovered.

"I love you," she sobbed, clutching me. The words weren't new. She said it over and over and often. We hadn't talked about why she'd gone home the day before. Her tears rolling down my arms and chest, I suddenly had to sit up. Everything, every thought, was bigger. It seemed like my head could crash through the ceiling if I stood up too fast. I sat up in the bed because suddenly I was seeing their marriage portrait. I'd ignored it until now, or it was there for tiny seconds, little bits. Only once, with my hands on it too, when she'd gone to the bathroom, and I got up to see it close. She'd hidden it under a layer of blouses on a junky, child-size set of drawers. I didn't look long because I couldn't, and I didn't want her to catch me. Framed in polished tin, both of them, I only really saw him in the blur of my curiosity. He was even blurrier in my memory. His black dress charro shirt with white stitching and buttons, his black hat with a silver studded band. His face didn't smile. It was carved as rough as Gerónimo's, but it was alive, too, like Juanito's. Its pride and confidence as harsh as a glare. That was what made me sit up: the image, not for prayer or fantasy, was pulling at me to stand. Below, I felt Isela tugging at me. She wanted me to lie back down, to hold her. She loved me, she said. "I love you, too," I said, kissing her like she was mine.

The Ceiba

CHINTO MOVES LIKE SOUND THROUGH EARPLUGS. Coming through the selva, lush at the back of my casita, his shoes grinding over the pebbles of a narrow path, branches scratching and leaves startled as he brushes against them. I can hear all of it, but not like the birds or a breeze. Suddenly he appears, I see him. Hidden in green shade, I never talk to anyone else—that's why I came here—and I don't want to talk to him now. Or ever really, although I am relieved when he's around. He's my only friend here. Still, I don't even want to see him until I'm forced to—and not up close, where he sees me, too. Maybe it's the steaming microbes everywhere that sag me. He's aware of how I am, how I react to him, and he keeps his distance before approaching too near. He allows himself the space to back away easy, smoothly, in silence, so that we can both pretend the encounter didn't happen. But I saw him, and he saw me see him.

When he talks it's barely audible, like he doesn't want to disturb nearby insects or birds.

"Chinto," I say. My look asks what is it he wants.

Cautious as any animal, he gauges first, deciding whether to come closer.

"All good?" I ask. "You fine?"

He shifts forward. "Yes, very fine." But only a few little steps forward. Which is as close as he will get, and not because I smell like I need a shower.

He usually wants me to give him some work to do. I try to think of things, though I don't think well, which isn't his fault. It is his sorry burden, it seems to me, that he has to ask for work from me. He's hungry.

"Everything back home is all right?" I ask.

He'd told me his wife and children were hundreds of miles from here.

"La ceiba," he says as if it were the only topic. "It's dead."

He and I had talked about this sacred tree, una ceiba, many months ago. It was because another man had come around. His full name, as he addressed himself, reduced to Nino—facially scarred, dirty skin and clothes, wearing sandals, but as smooth-talking as any hard-hatted white man from an engineering group—said he took dead trees, cut them up for leña. He would take the wood, but also wanted to get more for bringing down this tree, una ceiba.

I didn't like to talk to anyone back then either, though I wasn't as bad then as I am now. Still, I didn't trust him. How was he able to determine with certainty that the tree was dead? And how did he get back there to find out, why did he come from that direction, from behind my casita? Fence or no fence, was he just ignoring the privacy of the space around my little house?

Chinto lived nearby, I didn't know where exactly, and he always came from the back. So that, he, was okay, because it was him, and he was part of where I lived. Chinto didn't have anything to say when I saw him and asked about Nino.

I told him I did think the tree could be dead, but I didn't trust the man. Chinto said that he was someone he had worked for sometimes, but he agreed with me that there was something about him. And he didn't think the tree was dead. A ceiba tree was valuable to God, he told me as if just between us. He wanted the tree to live, swore he'd revive it.

That was before. Not anymore.

"In these rains," he says, meeting my eyes.

The tree was leaning toward the room with my bed. Which was really one whole side of the casita.

"Why is it dying?"

He had no answer.

"Wouldn't be good if it fell. On the house."

He seemed to agree. Though maybe he wanted to get work, money.

The casita had a tin roof. The wooden studs of two walls weren't chosen for permanence, for weight bearing, but as some kind of shoring up. Two other walls, away from any falling ceiba tree, were made of cinder block. Couldn't have been the ceiba tree, but something had happened before.

"Has to be done then," I said.

I assumed he'd do it himself somehow. He'd say yes to anything. Yes, he would, yes, he could, yes. Whatever, when he was doing whatever it was... he meant well, he worked hard in his way, but everything took more time because it was him. He didn't have say a screwdriver until I found him one. If I said, yes, good idea, fix that, sure, he'd also need me to have a hammer, and the nails, and the wood, and a ladder. Which meant I participated too. Which was not what I wanted.

I was good when he said he couldn't cut the ceiba down. He said that that Nino could though.

"If he still wants the work," I say, "tell him yes?"

Chinto was pleased. Maybe because it would mean some work for him with Nino and me. The assignment itself was a paid job for Chinto. He'd get on it. I didn't know what his end of this should cost me. I gave him a little here, a little there. I never knew what to pay him for being around for anything. For being this only friend of mine.

* * *

I was relieved to be back inside my little house, as if I'd been away for a long while even if it was only fifteen minutes. All was as it should be. I breathed in the fan air. Myself now. My strategy has been to lay low as much as possible, as long as needed, wait until I have the confidence to emerge healed or cleansed or whatever is demanded. I don't know. I admit it, and I'm not unaware that my success doesn't seem likely if judged by appearances. I don't like to cut my hair. It's worse than uncut, with only a comb to groom. I prefer to go shirtless and barefoot whenever possible. I wear soccer shorts without underwear and consider no shorts but...too unsanitary for me even. I am beginning to reason inappropriately about how often I trim my nails, like even where the clippings go matters. And I am beginning to believe it makes sense to be as I am. I wash myself with as little soap as possible, not wanting to leach the natural oils of my pelt, skin. I only worry about my odor when I have to be on the other side of the doors, in the world out there, near others. In here, it's hot. I sweat. I peel down to the least interferences.

Though I dislike the mosquitoes, I love the rain. A ferocious wind of hot downpour, heavy spouts of water plummeting down like waterfalls; thunder ancient, lightning immediate, a clatter like stones on the tin roof. I pull up shades to the smearing gray. Beauty so fierce is short-lived. Like all beauty.

The idea is to think around words and sentences. Castigations and aspersions, for example, need to be dismissed, not transcended, not escaped from as root and vine have to burrow and climb, leap, go around. More like air. The idea is to make it all like air. To make what is not seen as important as the visible.

Being here is moving on. Not running. This, here, what I'm doing, is backing away. Remembering? Though not what I'd prefer to call it, hiding is what it seems. I know what I can and can't do. I believe I know when I have the odds, when I don't, what's smart, what isn't. When to go back as far as I can, when to emerge.

I do push-ups, up to 500 in a set. It did cause pain at first. I learned to breathe and strain through and I found I could go even more, no physical need to stop except that it seemed reasonable I ought to. The same with crunches, thrusts, squats, bends. I stretch and curl and roll. It might seem like I dance. It isn't but I wish. Music is the birds and insects, now and then a distant voice or a loud radio that isn't as loud here inside, only everything that's out there, somewhere, not that far away really. There's the wind tangling in the trees and underbrush, the rain's dripping beats. I shower in unheated water. I eat any fruit and nuts and grains mixed at the mercado. I eat boiled chicken with tortillas from a comal. I live perfectly except for those few mosquitoes that I kill when I need to. I believe this is what I need and that I am lucky. I am in this little house. I am relearning.

* * *

I maintain the routine so...routinely, and I don't know how many days have passed without calculating. My hair grows. It seems to do this suddenly, it's not just that I only notice once in a while. I am not Chinto. Of course I will have to go out there again, presentably, I know this. I have to find out when, because of course I will have to. When I consider these needs, I think of laundry, clean shirts and pants that need ironing. Socks. Polished shoes. The hair even washed with shampoo, and cut. Perfumed oils rubbed in. A sharp razor to scrape off the hairs on my face, not just small scissors. Nails uniformly curved into a garden of fingers. I have to recall scenes, ways of speaking, rules of conversation. People will expect me to be pleasant and pay attention to them and not be distracted, elsewhere, seeing from a distance. A cafecito right there on the table. In a luminous ivory cup, its sheen so alive and fluid black as it ripples, a mercury of silver light, almost searing the retina.

I hear Chinto sweeping on the other side of the window. I don't want him. My broom? Or the palm fronds tied to a stick he sometimes uses? He needs money, that's not something wrong with him. It's only that I don't like even him to know I'm here, I don't like for anyone to even think I'm here. I don't want to be out there, but I don't really want to be in this casita if he knows I'm here. I don't know where I can go. There is nowhere for that. Has to be this way now, is all. He knows I'm here. Others can, do.

That sweeping sound has an insistence, a pleading. It's his way of knocking at the door, of checking in with me, of getting, besides money, information from me and passing information to me. I'm not sure what to do. I don't want to talk. I don't want to talk to him. To anyone. I know it's me. I do have to pay him to be here, to sweep. I do want to help him. I don't

98

want him to not be around. I want him to have food and shelter and all that his family needs. But I can't. He can't expect me, there's no way he can ask me. He knows, he must know. But he has to, like I have to open the door and talk to him. I really do like Chinto. He is more than kind. He takes me as I am. We did used to talk when I first came here. Friendly, sharing. Not groaning laughter, but cheerful smiling, contented. It's all me, I know this, but it's all me now who says it's him. That I feel him there so much. Around. More than the rain, more than wind. Like a shadow, he's not what you see unless you look down.

"Are you good, Chinto? How goes it?" I'm faking. Or I'm being what is normal, which clearly I am not now. I'm playing the opposite of what's me. I stand away from my open door, I never invite him to step in. "Did you hear back from Nino yet? He coming to make a pile of leña?"

I'm staring out from this door, into a dense, demanding green everywhere—sunless, without yellows—behind him and all around, so that it's hard to see his face.

"He's coming," Chinto says. "But"—he looks away guiltily, as though something bad were going to occur and it was his fault—"he says you have to pay him to cut it down."

"I thought he would do it for the firewood."

Chinto won't look at me as he speaks. "He says to cut it down, because it is una ceiba. Even though it is dead. He worries because it is a ceiba, and he wants to get money. Then he'll cut it for it leña and take it away, he says." This time he looks at me convincingly. "He'll bring his truck," he tells me like it's a secret.

We both hear the water dripping off the roof. We both turn our eyes to the dead tree as though it were teetering a little more than the last time. It is a big tree. A lot of work to bring down.

"Give me a minute?" I say. I'm barefoot and in my soccer shorts staring at a dying ceiba tree that...can fall any moment? Roots rise from the soggy ground uphill, opposite the lean. Talk of leña reminds me to gather some cash for him. I get a few bills and give them to him. He doesn't quite say no as he accepts them, but every other part of him apologizes for taking it, needing. His reluctance, even as it's the obvious reason he comes, makes me trust him.

"Seems necessary," I tell him finally. "Ask him, please, and as soon as he can. I don't want it to fall."

* * *

At the window I never stare long. I refuse to surrender the height or width of my attention. I sneak it in. And not the entire window, and never the middle of it either. I take in an edge, like a crack, and I only go up close for seconds when I do. If seen, I want it to seem like I'm doing something else. I let in just enough light as is needed so I don't have to use electricity, and because it stays cooler, and so on. I notice these dark blots sometimes. Birds flying by mostly. Only once in a while a human shadow. Which of course makes me curious and alert. I live so far away you'd think I'm not only safe but I'd feel safe. But everything and anybody is too close, no matter how far I go. That's it. I speak from experience. Whatever it is, whoever, can be right outside or even closer. A little is too much.

Like when I go to the mercado, I speak when I must, I listen. When I hear, it's really well. Each syllable and word and inflection of emotion or dialect or human puzzlement or social function. I hear so much more now. I see better too. Like an insect's eyes, mine flit over a wider band of color. I turn the slats of the wooden blinds upward so the light doesn't illuminate the floor. I'm surrounded by the chlorophyll of a thousand distinct shades of green. Blackened as an avocado skin here, bleached in a yellow sun there, brownish rich earth.

So now I had to go farther than the market. It took days. A tuk tuk ride, then a real taxi. Bright sunlight, muddy roads. Young women carrying wrapped babies, young boy walking crippled grandmother. The blind, the lame, the destitute. The very young screaming with joy. I too am happy as the tuk tuk putts back up the canopied hill to my casita. I pulled it off, no incidents, even if I caught the occasional skewed squint when someone suspected me just a little. My eyesight gasps as it readjusts to the rabid green. I can't wait to unpeel, be unlike those I've just come from. I want every whiff and smear off me. I want to pet and feed spiders and bugs. I want my naked feet to touch squishy soil and clay tile. I want to sweat like a swamp, shit and bury it like a cat. Or am I feverish? It does seem like it could be an illness. Could be return shock. Did I leave sick, or am I sick from there? My mind and body not sure which is which. Could be the wet, tidal heat, so deep and tall and churning?

Impossibly, as if he knew I was coming just then, Chinto arrives at my door at the exact moment as I do, a shadow behind me, even at midday when there is none.

"Chinto, you scared me!"

He doesn't know what I'm saying or why. He makes an uncertain laugh.

I don't laugh and I mean it, and he sees that. So he stands uneasy, weaving, like my words might strike him.

"It's good to see you, Chinto. Thank you."

"Nino came three days ago," he says very formal, testing the statement.

"Already?"

"He was mad that you weren't paying him money. I told him you would be back right away."

"And you weren't lying."

"So I'll tell him you're here?"

There were so many birds screeching, and that loud radio, wherever it was, too loud, and weren't those creek frogs? I knew the mosquitoes were already swarming me so I didn't want to stand there long. "I don't feel good, Chinto. I'm sorry." I was trying not to say that I wanted to be alone. I wasn't sure if I was going to be sick or if I just needed to sleep.

"I promised him. He was mad, and he wanted me to pay him."

What I wanted was to close the door.

"He wanted *me* to pay him," he said again, in between mad and scared. "I couldn't pay him any money."

"You don't need to worry, Chinto. I'll get to him. It's why I went."

He showed a profile from a distant time, farther than I was in my faraway. "If I'd had the money," he said, "maybe I would have had to."

"I got it, Chinto. Thank you so much. But not today. Tomorrow. Okay?"

What I don't ever miss is the everyday salt of anger. The need for a pinch here, some there, or much more, too much, too little. The fight inside that. The craze, the trance. The life or death, the all or nothing, the me or you, the winner loser. All the foolishness we create. What I miss are the bright splashes of joy, the waves of love, that thrill of a curve, the babies of small kisses. I miss what falls from a hazy, mystic cloud onto me, into me, my dry heart freshly watered, blooming.

The leaning, dying ceiba is gone now. And I feel it gone. Like my casita has shifted. I don't feel well.

I have to get away from me. Where? I have to not do this either. But first I want sleep. I'm tired, that must be why I feel sick. A little feverish but the heat is exterior, on the skin, the fervor of out there, not coming from inside me like it seems. Listen to the pattern of the drips, the slowest leak. I am so far away, and nobody but Chinto knows I'm here.

I think my heart is pounding, alerting me for some looming surprise. Then I understand it's the front door. I'm disheveled in my brain, body near naked, layered in too warm sweat. I don't even remember taking the other clothes off.

It is Nino, as bold in conviction as he is beating on my door.

"I need my money, sir."

"Excuse me," I say. "What time is it?"

Chinto is behind him, conflicted about his support. He wants to tell me the hour, even though I'd say he doesn't know it either.

"I am up in the morning," Nino tells me. "We get up for our work. I am here to get paid for the work I did here."

"I know what you want," I snap back. "I don't like you...treating me impolitely." I do not feel right. "Where do you think you are?"

"Sir, I expect to be paid for my work right here, where I am."

"But this isn't how," I say. "I don't like this."

I slam the door on him and then I am in a blank, pacing from here to there. And it worked. He doesn't pound the door again, he doesn't break it down.

It is steamy hot. The fan does nothing but add to my confusion and alarm, and I turn it off. I begin staring from the other side of the back door, outside, walking to where the tree was, the amputated space pulling me in. And then Chinto is beside me. He doesn't look at me.

"He took the leña, no?" I say. "To sell, no?"

"He wanted the leña," he says. A statement, it ended more as a question, one having nothing to do with the wood.

Barefoot, raw, an animal with an untranslatable gibberish language. That was me. There I was. Chinto was next to me, and his look was his, about him and his life. That caught my attention. He was no shadow. But mosquitoes were eating me up. I rushed inside.

* * *

The magueys had been planted on this side of the little house as a shield and boundary. They had grown enormous in this land where they didn't belong. They almost didn't seem to be agaves because their fattened hojas were too succulent. The plants were at least five feet in span, at least four feet high, and their tip thorns were comparably giant hard needles. You stayed away from them, you went around, you traversed carefully near them. Three of them had been crushed, near flattened.

"I knew there was something he did wrong, didn't I?" I tell Chinto. "He wanted me to pay him before I learned of it." It stank of lying. Even for this leña business, with so little at stake. "Who else would have done it?"

I'd never stood here, out in the open for anyone to see me. I was covered—long pants, shoes with socks up my ankles, long sleeves. I wished I could mask my face more because, though I couldn't hear the mosquitoes, every once in a while I'd feel one. My hands got bites near my knuckles. My neck was a target, and one bite swelled like an itchy boil.

"His truck ran over them. Look how big these agaves are. Couldn't have been a car, a taxi."

Chinto wasn't taking a position. But if the day before he'd seemed introspective, today he was lethargic, not right. He looked hungry, in need of vitamins. There was the heat, the rain, the throbbing green, but there was always Chinto. He was always. Not like this man. He seemed crushed, too.

"You didn't see it? When he was here?"

He shook his head

"You weren't around the day he came?"

"I didn't see this."

I couldn't understand. But it made me think of him again. "Are you okay, Chinto?"

"Yes, yes. Yes." He said this without inflections, like they were sounds, not responses.

My brain quieted. Neither of us did or said anything for a while, standing there with magueys, dead and alive.

"Listen, "I said. "Tomorrow, with a wheelbarrow, we can clean up here. I mean *we*. I can help. It's a lot of work for one man, for you with no help."

He was not fast or slow.

"Yes?" I said. "Can you find a carrucha? Or do we need something else?"

"Tomorrow I'll do it."

"I'll pay you, don't worry," I said uncomfortably. "You know that."

He grimaced. I couldn't determine if it was about doing this work, the money, or for some other reason.

He upset me. I remembered I was still a little nauseated. That I needed rice and beans at least, but I wasn't hungry. I didn't speed through so many ideas. I lost track of my feet. It was still hot, I was hot. I could feel it under the skein of clothes. I unbuttoned steadily. I untied laces and rolled off socks. I showered. The water, naturally tepid, cooling. I felt like I needed to be clean. I was neither sleepy or wide-awake when I stepped out of the bathroom. I put on semi-dry, washed soccer shorts. I pulled up the blinds in the back of the casita—I never opened these—and I began to see the outside darkening. The absence of the ceiba tree offered more open air to see through. More emptiness. It was as though I could hear the heat roaring like swarming insects.

I was out here as promised. I wanted to help. I didn't want to leave the maguey corpses to rot. I had a shovel. Dressed the same as always, a thin white T-shirt, jeans, a straw hat, Chinto came with a frail, old wheelbarrow and a machete to hack off the hojas one by one. We decided we could bury it all in the back, not far from the tree stump. We would replace them with baby shoots from the other plants, which grew often.

Chinto was super slow. He was having trouble cutting into the huge, tough leaves. At first I thought his blade might not be sharp enough, not a problem with his own strength. Then I thought that if it were that, then I didn't want it to be any sharper since he was swinging it so loosely.

"Are you sure you're okay, Chinto?"

"Yes," he said with disinterest. "Yes."

Not a true answer.

He insisted that I could not use the machete.

"Is there a place we could get lunch when we're done?" I wasn't hungry, I wasn't eating much either, but I could see he really needed food, not just lunch. We had never come close to sharing words let alone lunch. "Are you hungry?"

He had to have heard me. I waited and was about to repeat myself.

"Paches."

Did he mean he had these little tamales or wanted them?

I wasn't able to do a whole lot either. At the rate we were going, this could take days. We weren't half done burying the first one.

"Have you heard from Nino?"

He shook his head. We proceeded. The birds, the insects, then in what seemed a while, a big enough pile of chunks of hojas, and my job was to toss them into the wheelbarrow and drop them into the hole we'd dug.

He was only wounding the flesh of another huge hoja. It was one at the base, near the crushed piña. Bare earth was sighted.

"Look," he said alarmed. The word blew out of him like a surprise even to his own body. We both saw a fresh chunk of wood, from the ceiba tree. It was an irregular piece of leña, cut on three sides by a chain saw, its shape now a huge diamond's.

"Now you can believe me."

Easy to figure: Nino had backed up his truck into the road loaded with the leña that was once a ceiba tree. As he pushed through the resistance of the maguey, the cutting tumbled out. It was a kind of redemption for me—for me privately, yes, I needed to redeem myself, my anger, to Chinto's mind, about me, even if I seemed a little off, it wasn't about everything.

He held the chunk up with a strange admiration, as a wonder. For me it was more an archeological remnant, a museum piece. To him, a beautiful crystal. We took to the shade, to our bottles of water. A celebration. We both gave in to the day.

"Let's get something." I hadn't been anywhere since I was in the casita and never considered going anywhere with him.

He lowered his head.

"Chinto, what is it? You sick? Hot?"

"Maybe the dengue," he says.

I'm floored. I'd heard of it, of course, but it'd never crossed my mind that here, him. "You think you have it, or you were told you do?"

He didn't seem to know.

I believed it was something. Maybe dengue, but maybe something like it, less serious or more. "Do you know what to do? Do you need to go somewhere?" I meant a doctor, clinic, a hospital.

"I have to get over it," he says almost inaudibly.

I wanted to back away from him. I didn't want him to exhale air I might inhale. "A doctor first. I will help, I can pay for that."

His eyes pivoted, but only to the corners of mine.

Even if dengue spread by contact, when he handed the diamond leña to me, that wouldn't be the most likely route it'd take. Dengue came by way of mosquitoes, and that means you have to get bitten by mosquitoes. If he were right, if he'd gone to an actual doctor, if it was dengue. But it felt like I had some of it too. Something. I was already sick when I arrived. Even before? How long had I been, call it, feverish? What was the fever, what me? Maybe I even gave it to him. Not just now, but weeks before. Incubating that long? Or a lot of mosquito bites? Or was it the swampy heat, this wanton green.

Inside I put on long sleeves and pants and shoes. I slept with a mosquitero. I heard the buzz everywhere, louder than frogs and birds and crickets and that distant or too close radio. I wandered around outside—I hadn't paid much attention to where I was, this exact land I lived on, its details and contours—searching for Chinto when the days began to pass and he didn't come. The dead, giant magueys, their hojas wilting and seeping, were binding to the soil. I worried and I looked for him behind and in front of my casita. Nobody near my little house—shaded people and shaded places I had been barely conscious of—knew where he'd stayed or lived if they even knew him at all. I listened for him, my ears squinting through the rage of life around me because Chinto made so little sound. Now there was nowhere near or far to go, and no one else, only me.

Wilshire and Grand

USUALLY I DROVE BY OLD JOBS EVERY YEAR OR SO TO see what was new around them, to certify they were still standing. There was always something specific to squint at, a small almost nothing cosita. One building at 3rd and Hope, all poured-in-place cement, had leaned an inch and a half out of plumb by the ninth floor, so we had to get it right in the next two pours. That was me and Hector. It must have passed inspection since I never heard anything when we topped off at thirty-two. I go and stare up to see that fat lip we left. My work. That company got me three years. It was a good gig. I had a few like that. I'd say one in three made me like being in the trades, proud of what I did for a living.

I didn't like remembering this one at Wilshire and Grand. It was the kind that turned you into a slinky tarantula. After a bad period at the hall, I'd come onto the job relieved it looked like one that could keep me going up to a year. The fucked-up part was the nalgón who came out of the hall with me. A foreman takes you on with a dude and they think the two of you are born together. I don't like expecting to get fired. You never go to a foreman to bitch. Never works out. I did it anyway. I made that move a few weeks in, all hate-to-bother or say anything, sir. The foreman, a quiet man—which is why I decided to take the risk, that he wasn't the usual culo—didn't even respond any way bad. No frown, sigh, stare away, nada. He didn't ask for a full explanation, a story, any particulars. I just told him how it'd be better if we were working with different partners. His answer came a few hours later when he handed us both layoff checks. Problem solved. Pissed, I stole a sawzall on my way out. A heavy-duty Milwaukee, used but not old, long industrial cord. I tossed it in my toolbox on my walk-off. Fuck them, fuck this job. I hadn't driven by to see it once in all these years. I was there now because she suggested it.

I'd met her across the street, on Grand. A couple of us were having draft beers for lunch break. It wasn't a Starbucks back then. It had a mahogany bar and served swanky diner food. Had a vinyl booth up against tall glass windows. The Chinese takeout also seemed to have moved a couple establishments away. It'd been next door to the diner, or that's how I remembered it. And the deli was on the opposite corner, not next to this high-rise. I went there every day during and sometimes after work. Those mexicanos were the best for break sandwiches and burritos and doing beer runs for me, for us. They did lots for me because they loved my ass. Fact only. It was how I was back in the day. I opened the door, their smiles took over—my ease in English was power, my Spanish like we were all from the same big cornfield. I made them laugh. I was them if they could be tall and not afraid of migra vans. All probably a little too fun, and from this side, from this big city, and a Chicanito. They especially liked that word. Made them laugh and get excited, both what they wanted and what they never were going to be. They let me use their work phone for the movida I had going. How could they not? It was LA, I was LA. Not like I could call her from my own home. For them, she was *esa guëra*—singsong, like morning chirps—and me, I was *ese Lito*, like a mockingbird's hoarse echo.

All this time later and now here I was waiting for the same her. And I could see her like those dudes back then did. Her as more than too much. She was wet and tart with lime, stronger than mezcal, as foreign as French, and American as twenty-dollar tips. I remembered how she craved...what? Not sure really, then or now. I just went with it. She liked her own badness, a wild all hers. What a pendejo she made of me, I made of myself. And then I got fired from that puto jale.

Sitting at the Starbucks window now, the outside the same and not at all. It wasn't the first time she contacted me, only the first time I didn't say no thanks. Not because I wanted more trouble or needed to or couldn't not. Only because there was nothing, no good reason for no anymore. I'd become curious about my life, not hers. Probably because so much time had gone by and it never crossed my mind that...I never thought about life. The big picture. I'd just been living it one day to the next. Someone like her, her exactly, seemed like she had a plan, even a step one and a two. She made her life happen for her, not at her. I used to be pissed about that life of hers. I lose a job, she gets a cha-ching better one.

"Isn't this your order, sir?" said a scruffy man. He wore a Starbucks apron. "Carlos?" He pointed to the name written on the white cup. "That you?"

"I didn't hear anything," I said. My table couldn't have been closer to where all of the orders were called out. "Sorry. Thanks."

"De nada," the man said. He didn't look Spanish-speaking, he didn't sound Spanish-speaking. His words sounded more like he was mispronouncing someone's last name.

Another man in a green apron, a lot more ordinary, younger and neat, a manager type, approached hard. "Leave him alone," he told the strange man. His put his hand on the man's shoulder and gave it a push. "Come on, let's go."

"No!" The strange man hopped almost a foot backwards. Then he spun and rushed toward the front of the café by the door.

"He wasn't bothering me," I told the manager. "I forgot to pick up my order. I didn't hear it was ready."

The manager shook his head at me impatiently. "He doesn't work here. He took an apron and put it on." He started telling me, but talking somewhere else, they had all kinds of incidents with street people. He turned back to join a female employee behind the counter, and two more employees came too, one of them on the phone.

"I'm not leaving!" the pudgy strange one in the stolen apron shouted from the door.

They'd stopped making coffee and calling out names on cups. Customers at the front of the café hadn't particularly noticed a thing though. After enough seconds passed, the workers went back to it like at all Starbucks. Only this manager remained disturbed. I sipped. Good coffee! Close to the action, I was sipping more when the young manager—he looked twenty-five at most—came out of a corner with one of the young women employees, talking about how they might get the apron back. She thought the predicament was funny.

"Mi Lito lindo," Nikki said. She came up to me from where I wasn't looking. She was dressed like she was still in her late twenties, in a business sexy skirt and blouse, her hair highlighted in the latest, her lipstick a subtle pink.

"Mi Nikki nookie," I teased back like I used to.

We both laughed, the air responsible, not our comfort.

I stood for the obligatory hug. As I sat back down and took my eyes off her, I checked myself. Probably been better to not start right there.

"You look really good," she told me. "I don't know why I didn't expect that."

"Wow, thanks. I thought you'd look like crap too."

She laughed. The laugh was still her then.

"Really you don't," I said. "You know, look bad." It came out clumsy. "You look healthy, and... you look good, Nikki." I couldn't get anything out right. "A really nice dress, too..."

She was patient through it. "A pound more every year," she said. "And I don't count years either."

She waited.

"So you came back from New York."

"It was great for a minute. Too long there. At first I felt like I was in the big time. But I like LA."

"All seems pretty big time to a pinche Mexican like me. Though to me driving to Mexicali or Vegas is big doodoo."

She smiled, happy. "How could I not miss you?"

"Ay, look how good you make up words," I said.

It stayed there. It was nice there.

"Now you work right here again?"

"Not really. Close enough though. I don't have the garage parking over there now"—she nodded to some place out the window—"like before." She paused, remembering. "I'm close though." She looked out longer and farther away, then back at me.

Seemed like she was going to say something else. She'd invited me here for some reason.

"You look really good, Carlitos."

"Looking ain't everything."

She smiled. "So," she said, half asking, half saying.

"A little crazy," I said, "meeting up ... "

"Crazy was our thing!" she broke in.

" ... right here even," and then I got what she said seconds late. "Can I get you a coffee?"

"In a few," she said. She went quiet.

"It's really been a while," I said finally. "This is the first time I'm back. Hadn't even seen the higher half of that building that went up."

She stared out the window at what could be seen of it. All of it wasn't visible, only the lower half, the part from when I'd worked there. Which seemed kind of right. Not a fond memory though, and too much since.

"That fucken job," I said. Then, resentfully, "but it did turn out good for you."

I met her here, this hottie who wasn't afraid to flirt or drink. She claimed to be a writer. After a few times hanging out after work, she told me she was writing about my job building a high-rise. And me. Not about the *us* part. Not about me as a dog—or her in heat. No, about me as a Chicano, a union construction worker in LA, a native of the city. And she did that. She got to know more about my work, that job, from inside, than I ever did. About the union hall and my business agent there, about the super and the foreman who eventually laid me and the fatass off—she didn't tell them I was in her story or that she knew me personally. The pictures were really great, the story seemed like the centerfold of the magazine. It came out months after I'd been let go. I felt pretty *chingón* for a couple of weeks even if I was unemployed or doing small side jobs for some cash. My wife and kids thought I was a hero for about a month. It made me feel like I was going to be rich, something like that.

"You gotta be over it by now," she said.

"I couldn't find work for a year. And then everything else."

"It wasn't like it wasn't a little bit of your own making, Carlos."

"What's that mean?"

"There was your drinking at breaks. There was playing the babes at lunch. Smoking weed after work...late hours."

"With you!"

"Exactly. Like me when I came along."

I didn't know what I was talking about this pedo for, thinking about this way past past—or what I was doing here.

"I didn't know you were married," she said.

"You did too. I'll bet I even told you the first day."

Like she knew everything but she didn't know that? I was a little mad, but I wasn't getting mad like I used to. I noticed that. It caught my attention. I drank the good coffee as emphasis for her. A couple of sips.

"I did know," she confessed, "I did. You're right, that's true. I knew it."

Yeah, and I knew she knew it. But the so 'deep' honesty was a jolt.

"Wasn't this your idea?" I asked. "Us meeting?"

"It wasn't to talk about all that bs," she said.

"Yeah. All that mess is way over."

"I imagined it'd be sweet, even fun," she said. "You had fun before. *We* did. Come on."

I didn't say I agreed, I could have maybe, but...better to be changing the subject.

"Doesn't it seem a lot different here to you?" I asked. I nodded my head to the outside.

"The street? I guess I'd say no. The building you were at, kind of. But it wasn't close to finished back then. Time, nada más."

I hated that she added some Spanish. In the past, Spanish meant I was *in* with a white girl like her. A tell. Now, only aggravating. "Seems to me places aren't where they're supposed to be, where they were."

She made a face. "Sounds like an illness," she said, smiling. "I guess you aren't so perfect after all."

"Like here," I said, "this Starbucks. It used to be a restaurant. Where we met."

"Where you picked me up?"

"I forget. You didn't let me?"

"I think that restaurant is a little up the street on this block. An Irish pub still I think."

"No, that can't be right. There was a deli on the other corner, too."

"Or early onset Alzheimer's. Besides maybe never being here, places can move away or go out of business. If they existed."

"I remember it right across the street, here. I don't believe this isn't where. That I'd get it so wrong."

"Me either," she said, grinning.

"I don't have a good memory now?"

Suddenly both the high table we sat at and Nikki in her chair were sideswiped by the strange man in the Starbucks apron. The manager jumped around and tried to grab him again, and the man tumbled against their table, toppling over my coffee onto her dress, then shoving off her as he recovered. Stumbling sideways, he accidentally slapped another woman employee as he flailed his arms.

"What the fuck!" I was on my feet. His attention shifted fast to me. He bobbed like we were in a boxing ring, backing away. The manager kept a tense distance.

"Stay away from me, you stinking wetball! Go back to where you came!" Slobbish and soft, his movements were electric, his feet dancing stupidly and hands fluttering. And then, like that, he whipped around and fled to and out the glass door of the café once again.

"You all right?" I asked Nikki.

"Just coffee," she said.

"Fucken nuts!" I said.

"I'm so sorry," said the manager.

"I'm okay," she said.

"You could've fallen," I said. "She could've been knocked over," I told the young woman employee.

"Almost," Nikki said. "I'm okay though." She started patting her dress with a napkin.

The woman brought over a stack of them.

"Should we leave?" I asked.

"Can I get you both coffees? Anything?"

"Or we can leave," I told Nikki.

"Let's give it a few," she said. "Get myself back together." She was still dabbing the coffee from her dress with water. "I invited you!"

We laughed. I ordered coffees.

"Wow," I finally told her. The same table, like nothing happened except for her stained dress and an extra coffee.

"Never a dull moment with you around," she said.

"He ended up blaming whatever it was on me. What's that?"

She laughed lightly. "Wetball."

"That was a new one."

"And you didn't...I don't know, react. The old you, the Chicano I knew, would be running at him, beating him down *con chingados*."

I shook my head, sighed and groaned, but only inside. Was it only because now that I was older, all these things repeated so many times, so many ways?

"*Chingazos*," I corrected her.

"Yes, yes of course!" she said. "I'm a dummy."

When I was younger, I liked R&B oldies. Smokey Robinson, Mary Wells, Sam Cooke. Lots of us did. That was the music for our types those days. And I clearly wasn't Black.

"He got his racist shit words all confused," I said. "Mixed greaseball and wetback."

"I like wetball better," she said.

"I guess it does have a new ring to it," I agreed.

She was one hundred percent done swabbing her blouse and skirt. It seemed calm.

"So what are you doing these days?" she finally asked. "How's your union?"

I stopped working for the union not that long after. First I broke a foot. Then tore an Achilles. Then I worked on a crew that installed commercial windows. I couldn't take it. I went from gig to gig. My wife remarried, my kids grew, a few girlfriends came and went. I lived cheap in South Gate. I practically never came to downtown LA anymore.

"Is that why we're here? Another magazine article? What do they call those? A follow up?"

"Carlitos," she said sadly. "If you're not kidding, that's really dumb."

She was right, I should've been joking around. At least should've sounded more like I was. But that time—"A Chicano Climbs High," a photo of me hanging off about ten floors, a sledge in my hand—and she gets todo everything writing about us. I got one gig out of the hall that only lasted three weeks. But ya, I had to stop.

"I got fired at this job, man. Sitting here, seeing it and going back, still pisses me off. Not on you. Sorry."

"I'm sorry," she said. "It's so many years ago to me. It didn't cross my mind that it might still...still be something to you."

"It's stupid. My stupid." I stopped. "I swear to God that restaurant was here. It was here. Right across the street from that jobsite."

"If you insist," she said, shaking her head.

"The Chinese joint? The deli?"

She shrugged. "The restaurant is maybe only a hundred, two hundred feet from here. An easy mistake. If I'm right."

"I guess I can walk by after," I said, surrendering to end it. "I probably got all kinds of shit wrong."

I saw myself wearing a faded serape. Back then she saw me as some kind of movie-star charro on a white stallion prancing beneath her bedroom window. And I felt as strong, bigger than life, as heroic as what she saw in me, what she wrote about me. Now I was just a poor old Chicano, barely getting by.

"What about you? Besides work, what's with you? Married, divorced, both, neither? Babies? Puppies? Probably lots of boyfriends, with or without a husband."

She shook her head again. "Let's not go there. I'm good though. I only wanted to see you again."

"Here," I said. "At the Starbucks. Where we never met."

She really laughed. "I've missed you, Carlitos."

It occurred to me that she was serious.

"I totally get that," I said. "From a lot of practice, because I gotta be careful with hot gold diggers."

She laughed harder. That killed enough time for me to appreciate the fine coffee again—I never bought fine coffee. "Don't laugh at me if I tell you?" she asked.

That made me laugh.

"Yes?" she asked.

"I'm definitely full-time serious listening now."

She was hesitating.

"Honest," I said. "I'm listening. I really do want to know what."

"Okay then. Short version first: I realized that I was in love with you."

My instinct was to joke. Smile it off anyway. Go *aww* or *qué loca eres*, something all smart like that. Maybe this proclamation could make someone else feel very happy? She was a beauty. She had everything, and would get all the rest, too. And here she was talking to *me*, saying this. Which was my fear: I didn't know who the hell she was and did we ever meet before? I wasn't even sure I was ever here in this place now called Starbucks before.

"I know what you're thinking," she said, "but I mean it." She gazed over at me, in that way that meant she meant it. "I was in love with you back then. Real love. I know you didn't have any idea of it. I was certain that wasn't even close to what you were feeling. It was chaotic, wild, so fun, but I knew it. I wanted it not to be true. I knew it was wrong. Your children alone..."

I forgot we were in a Starbucks until I took a sip of that good coffee.

"But these last few years, I've been wanting to tell you. To ask you."

I sort of nodded. Ask me? And who knows, maybe I would have been able to respond, or hear more, who knows, but suddenly, out of nowhere, my tall stool and I went mobile. I was smashed into head-on, the stool beneath me sliding some distance until it tipped over, hurling me off beyond it.

Seemed like no one had seen the pudgy street dude with the stolen smock come back through the door charging at me full force. From the floor, once I got my bearings, I could hear screaming and yelling but no words. He was down at first, too. It was Nikki who was confronting him as he stood up near me. He had that same frantic shake of energy, he was about to make another move, when her right leg swung. She crushed his manhood, and as he bent over in agony, she left-hooked his face. You would think that would have ended it. I was standing again, unsure if anything hurt, though I seemed fine to me, when he got his wind back—and even with so many people around him, he blew by all of them and sprinted out the door yet again. There was so much yelling and loud talking, I couldn't hear what Nikki was saying to me.

I wanted air around me. I didn't want to be hugged by anyone. But Nikki wanted to and what could I do?

"I'll be fine," I told her. "I am fine. No injuries."

"Let them take you to the hospital," she said. "I'll go with you." She was worried, caring. "If you want," she added quickly. Another sort of worry.

LAPD officers were coming through the door.

"I don't want that," I said. "You sure did kick that fucker where he won't forget," I told her. "I'd never guessed you were such a badass."

"You have to go get checked out," she told me. "Your head hit hard."

The cops came up to us. The one talking told us an ambulance was coming.

"I'm all right," I told him.

"He needs to be checked on," she said. "Just go to the hospital!"

"No," I told her and both cops.

She stared at me, mad and hurt both.

It was hard for me to understand, let alone explain, and I couldn't and wouldn't try.

She didn't say anything to me while she waited for more. When there wasn't anything, she turned to the LAPD officers. She didn't look back at me once she got with them about what had happened.

I didn't know if I was in the restaurant where I first saw her. I didn't know if I deserved my barely making it, messy life, or if it was because I had to get along with culos who I refused to treat as an equal. I couldn't be positive if this smart beautiful güera with the silky, pinkish lipstick was anyone I had known before today, or if I was only a fantasy she had, a false memory, of mine, or hers. The deli I went to back then, those mexicanos, always happy, working all the time for cash, off the books, all hours, right there, or over there?

I walked to the glass door and out. Nobody, no customers or employees, not even the young manager, seemed to see me whatsoever. I stopped in front of Wilshire, and I turned right on Grand. I began slowly, trying to recall exactly where I'd parked—was it in the direction that she said was the Irish bub?—when, whooshing by me, flew an amber beer bottle. It missed my head by I'd guess one foot, plus or minus, and smacked the tall, thick tinted glass pane of the Starbucks behind me. It didn't break that window, though the bottle shattered when it rebounded off and hit the cement sidewalk. The pudgy street dude, a few steps off the other sidewalk opposite me on Grand, screamed: "Get your Mexican outta here! Go home, you beaner grease!" And then he took off hard, running twice as fast as he should have been able to. Four cops raced out of the café to chase him.

Faces were breathing close to the tinted windows of Starbucks, their eyes popping and mouths wedged open by the spectacle. I was standing there, blank, readying for the long walk on a dirt trail with a loaded burro.

Deal

QUE PASÓ, BRO, DRU SAYS, SMILING. HOW YOU BE, mister E?

What up dude, E says on auto reply.

Not too much, not too much. Dru's on the flyer crew, and right then the rigger and crane were moving a section, just cleared out, up to this floor. He was only half paying attention to what was around the jobsite. Dru wasn't one of the men who landed the flyer and set it, only once it was ready for steel and forms.

Got some talk for ya, he says.

I'm here now, bro, E says. Make it later.

E is at the top of a column, he and his partner Doc are plumbing the column. The job's right downtown LA, very close to the Harbor Freeway. They're on nine, sixteen floors to go. The pour is the next day. E's been on this job almost two months. He'd been out of work for longer.

At morning break Dru, alone at a distance, waves E over with his eyes and head motion. E was sitting between the Spanish-speaking laborers and a handful of carpenters, white guys except his partner MD, "Doc." He'd been a Compton high school running back—that was about all he knew personally about his partner. Hungry, E was eating a chorizo and egg sandwich and didn't feel like going over to him but if he didn't....E doesn't want Dru making noise his way, calling out for attention. He takes the sandwich he's eating and leaves the other and makes it seem he's going to the pisser.

What up? E says.

That were good shit, bro, Dru says.

His mouth full, it was easy to nod. Cool, glad, he says.

I knew you come through, Dru says.

E nods his head.

No doubt, Dru says.

E nods a little less. He had maybe two bites left.

Some doubt, says E.

He makes it one bite, all in.

I knew you have them...mex connects, Dru says. He laughs. Shit were good. And good price.

I'm still hungry, bro, says E. He points to his watch. I need to get me another.

Yeah yeah, one second. What you say if I get fifty?

E doesn't know what to say.

Fifty ain't too big and not so little to be more good, says Dru. Lemme hear back.

After work, before he gets to his place, E stops at the corner store near his El Sereno home and buys a cold six and pops one. Parked he calls his cuñado Jimmy.

Are you crazy? Jimmy says.

Just thinking about it.

I thought you said that one was a favor.

I did.

What's this about?

Money. You know that.

I thought you said unión feria was like, you know, wet.

I don't gotta bank.

I shouldn't feed you, man. You grow.

But you can get it? Same shit?

Jimmy doesn't respond fast. Pretty sure, he finally says.

Pretty sure?

Seems to be going fast. But they'll have better if anything.
I'm thinking it out.

Your dude's good for it?

Pretty sure.

Pretty sure?

Yeah. But my worry, still thinking, we'll see.

I dunno, E. I don't want no trouble at our cribs.

I know I know. I'll get back at you.

Bueno pues, your deal.

* * *

E and Jimmy grew up together in El Paso since elementary school. E a small house on quiet Idalia, Jimmy's room in a casita with his grandparents from this side, behind a rowdy bar near Copia and Pershing that his uncle owned. He was in Juárez a lot, a big messy family. They were closer than most brothers. When Jimmy did some business in LA way back, he met Ali. She went crazy for him like all girls and then women did. Jimmy stayed longer for Ali. E decided to see LA when he could easy while Jimmy was there. He fell in love with Ali's sister Aurora. The two sisters were both pregnant the same month.

* * *

E got home with four of the six left.

Nayeli was by the stove. Hey baby, she says, seeing the beer. It was a good day?

It's Friday, E says. He didn't usually buy beer on the way home. You? You okay? He puts them in the fridge, takes one.

She leans against the sink opposite the old stove, watching a pot of beans simmer. You don't work tomorrow? That's what the beer usually meant.

Of course.

That seemed to make her sadder.

Maybe not all day, he says. We need the money, right?

That didn't help.

What is it? He puts his arms around her. You keep being like this.

You stink!

He unhugs, begins to back off.

No, she says, pulling him close. Then she starts crying.

Tell me.

It's nothing.

She holds him hard. They can feel each other.

Take a shower, she tells him quietly. Meet me in bed.

But..., he starts.

Bobby's with Fausto. Suzy's staying the night at Gabriela's.

They both still looked good naked. They both wanted each other's bodies like they were surprised. She liked his mouth on her breasts like a need she had. He liked feeling the curves from her waist to her hips as though that was where it happened. She liked having him inside from on top, eyes closed, surrounded by pulsing stars, and he loved watching her body writhe like it was so unexpected, too much pleasure.

My god I love you, she says. I wanted you all day.

Just think if we weren't married.

Shut up. What's that mean?

I'm joking.

Stupid. Stupid to say.

They say it's not as good once you're married. Just think what we must be missing.

Have you been talking to my sister's...her perro mujeriego?

Come on, I'm playing with you. Be nice.

She cuddles. Don't ever be like him. You're mine, nobody else's.

They get quiet, feeling each other again. At first came little tears, then she is crying.

What is it?

Nothing. I dunno. Nothing.

Gotta be something.

I don't know what's wrong with me.

You are being strange.

I know. It's everything.

You keep saying that.

Ali's going through the same thing. And I have you, not her man.

Stop. You always go there. I wish I could make half as much as Jimmy.

Until they lock him up again.

He's not doing shit now.

You don't know.

You do?

I know Ali worries.

Stop it.

It's true though. How can he be...

...making more than us? E says.

For one, sure. That's only one thing. He's never here.

He owns three bars there, and they're doing good. He's doing it with what he got.

Liquor, drugs, girls, Juárez, and El Paso.

It's where we're from!

E gets out of the bed and collects his clothes.

Nayeli sits up. Don't get so mad.

You just don't get it. He's doing what it takes. He's got less than nothing here in LA. He had nothing much there and now it's something. He wants better. He wants to be here all the time, wants his family here. We both want better.

He's supposed to live here, where his wife and children are.

You think he should just work for some pendejo and say a sus ordenes all day?

* * *

It is early morning, crisp air blue skies, the whoosh of distant freeway traffic like a desert wind. E is waiting on the concrete trucks to start pouring.

Que pasó, bro, Dru says.

Hey, what up dude? E wasn't expecting any talk by anyone.

Things happening, man?

E nodded. In a few days. I'll let you know.

Can you make it seventy-five? Things is dry.

E seems like he's listening more for concrete. I dunno. He isn't sure he should.

Things is dry, Dru says again. Demand is high, man.

You can do it?

I can do more, brother man. Can you do it?

E has to think. What he doesn't trust is the gaming. Dru's way.

You still have to handle half up front. You got that?

No doubt, no doubt man. All be done in a week. You watch.

It was so hard to resist. He was doubling his money as it was. Seemed so easy. And this job would end in a few months. What was good was that he didn't know this Dru, Dru didn't know him. That was bad too and could be worse. It wasn't that much, but a lot for him if it didn't go smooth.

I still want half up front.

Come on, E. Not my first ride, brother. It'll be good on both us.

I'll get back.

You'll see. Too little really. You don't gotta believe, you gotta know.

E calls Jimmy at lunch break. Jimmy had to front it all to E.

I can, Jimmy says, and I will, but I don't want to very much.

It's not that much more.

It's that these aren't the…how d'ya say…people I know. Gente decente…even if. They know me so todo'sta bien….

It'll go, I'll get it. He's okay.

E isn't really comfortable either, little as it was.

I'm not liking it. Not my tight circle.

If you can't…

You know I can.

…or if it's too much…

For you. Now.

…I just don't got any cash. Kinda why this.

I knew you when you were a baby. That was just a couple weeks ago.

E laughs.

All I need is something else for the A girls to hang on me.

They won't know.

This is it though, right? I mean, I'm not easy. Not the money, only doing biz like this. Little chiles burn hotter.

It ain't the money...well, course it is. But it's not too.

I get it. I know. Kinda what I'm saying.

I like my work, Jimmy. When it's good. But...I dunno. Fuck them. It's there. They got their mansions and Mercedes. I never saw mansions or Mercedes before I was here. I need a little cash.

Yeah.

Fuck them.

Jimmy laughs at him.

I gotta do something.

* * *

E was hitting balls for infield practice.

Come on, Fausto. Don't wait on it! Charge, throw it hard to first! He hit him another that took a hop on the dry, scarred field. Again! E says. He slapped it hard to Fausto's right, near the bag, and he handled it well but was slow to turn and throw. E hits another and Fausto handles it smoothly, but threw to first like he didn't give a shit. Then he gets a slower one, one he had to charge, and makes a lazy but okay throw.

Hit it to someone else, coach. He starts walking off the diamond.

What the hell you saying? says E.

That now you can hit it to short or second, to Bobby or Rene, not me. Fausto is already headed toward the dugout, to the water.

E, steaming, bangs a few at the other boys, then asks another dad, another coach who'd been hitting fly balls to outfielders, to take them all.

Fausto is in the stands.

What's your problem? E said.

Nothing. Fausto isn't backing down.

Nothing. Right.

I just got tired of it.

Ground balls?

I guess, yeah.

Or me on you?

Fausto looks at E. Because it's hot today.

I'm on you because you're our best player. You're the team, Fausto. All the others want to be you.

When did you get your tats, coach? How old were you?

Híquela. I was old, mijo. And I wasn't even in LA like you. I'm from the sticks. Even here you probably gotta wait a while.

My mom says only cholos have them. Pintos. Like my dad.

He was a cholo? A pinto?

He's a pinto.

That's not so good.

I was thinking I want them. They're showing up on everyone cool, güey.

E laughed. "Güey"?

Sorry, coach. They're just badass.

A few years, tal vez a couple a championships, get any you want. Your moms won't care so much then.

Maybe so.

Whadaya want? Where?

Right here on my arm first. A spider, maybe like a black widow. Or a scorpion, because I got bit by one once in México when I was little.

We got plenty of them in El Paso. One bit me on my face in bed.

Wow, reallys? Did it fuck you up, coach?

Nah, E says. I guess they do some people.

Badass.

Hey we should rename our team the Scorpions.

That would be badass, coach! The Lions kinda sucks.

I agree. Maybe I can next year.

That'd be really cool, lots better. That Lions name's older than the uniforms.

I'm getting us new uniforms.

Yeah, coach? When?

Maybe in a week or so, I'll see.

Fausto stood.

Mijo, you're our best player. You're really good, dude. You get after it, you push, you can be as good as they come. You're really good, man. You got it all. Remember that.

Okay, coach. Thanks, coach.

* * *

Only four days later E gets to work even earlier to see Dru ride in.

° Dru hands him an envelope folded. It's shy, brother E, but you don't got to worry.

Shy what?

All I got now.

Of what?

The half.

You mean it's not half? E looks around for crew parking, walking, any eyes nearby. He hates having to count cash and fast, and pissed, but no choice. You're saying it ain't half?

Yeah. Not yet. But it will be, E.

Fuck dude. Fuck. Really?

It was hundreds less than a fourth.

You caught me at a bad time, brother. I didn't expect it so fast.

The fuck man, you were in a mad rush.

I'll get it quick, you'll see. Fast. De valada, man. Serious.

Dru's bad Spanish pisses E more. He wants to think faster than he can. He doesn't want them talking too long, getting angry, seen and then talked about.

Fuck man, E says. I don't know.

In a couple days it'll look better. I couldn't tie it up after work yesterday is all.

You mean if we wait until tomorrow, you'll have all the half?

Dru is tongue-tied.

No is the answer to that, says E.

I gotta sell some to get you yours. It'll go fast, brother. You watch and see. A couple few days.

You said that. About fifty, then seventy-five.

And it true. All done in a couple few weeks, tops. Sooner!

I went to a lotta trouble. I got a no return policy.

You worrying, brother. Come on.

I got my end for the worry.

All will be good.

You told me it was like three four dudes.

And it is, it is like that.

E shifts his brain. We'll have to do whatever next at break. Too late now.

I'll say I'm going to the liquor store.

Maybe I'm giving you fifty now.

Whatever be good man.

And you come up with what's half *that* in a day or two?

Okay okay, you got it.

E steps out of his car, five minutes to start time. He's thinking maybe it'll have to be even less.

Lemme have that bread back then, Dru says.

What?

Til we do this, brother, that my bread.

E pulls the wad out and gives it to him.

They walk together for only a few yards.

Breaktime, E says as their space widens, separates.

Dru says not a word.

* * *

E opens the refri and takes out two beers.

Hey baby, Nayeli says.

He was drinking one.

Not a great day? Nayeli says.

Long pour day is all.

You hungry?

Not really. Not yet. He hears the TV. Bobby and Suzy are home.

I thought I'd get us pollo ranchero at that place we like.

E nods. He walks straight to the bedroom. So filthy, he knows he shouldn't fall on the bed. He can't stop or not shut his eyes. So sweet to lie down. It's almost like sleep, though it seems better. And maybe it is because he can only catch up with Nayeli talking once she's pushing at him. Take a shower! she's saying. He hears her saying his name. He pulls up his head, rolls on his back.

Maybe you do need to sleep, stinky, she says.

E's not ready to talk.

Nayeli holds him, almost snuggles. See, I love how you smell.

·

The Last Painting

EVERY FUCKEN *THAT* IS NOT *THAT*.

"Mande?" Gabriel said.

"What?" I said.

"Es que...you said something, y no lo...I didn't hear good."

Jesus, now when I think I'm only talking to myself, I'm not.

"Nada de importancia," I said. "Mumbling pedo. No dije nada, nothing."

Gabriel stared at me, mystified.

He was here to paint. We'd talked a few days before about which rooms. The price was super good, so I threw in a repaint of my living room. Two men, in two days, that was pretty great. He was supposed to start at nine and now it was almost two. It was supposed to be two men, now it was him and Gabito, his pre-teen son he introduced me to.

"I had to stop and buy the paint at the paint store," Gabriel said carefully, reading my irritated mind. "Traje..." he started in Spanish. "...I brought my son," he continued, smiling. "He's better than any man. He will help me, you'll see. My wife, she helps, and I thought she would come, pero she couldn't porque..."

"Just so you get the job done," I interrupted. "Seems like it will probably take more than the two days you said."

"No no, Mr Jacobo...."

"That's my first name. I go by Jake. My last name is..."

"...es *Caves*."

Gabriel thought that because I'd found him through my musician brother, Benny. Benny was in the band, in The Smudges, way back when we were big. Though not huge, ten years big ain't bad. And those dudes, crazy and talented white guys, liked calling me *Caves*. And they made that stick, and I guess I thought it was kind of...who-gives-a-shit cool. And so it got stuck on me for like forty years already in the world where I've made all my money and career. Though not most of my money. I did better than those other dudes. They would say, they would whisper a little too loud (pissed me off at the time—if popped, long prison time in Texas), Caves has connections to Mexican cuevas, jaja. What was true is that I knew gente in Juárez who knew peoples in...and so forth. I was la conecta in a big music scene world of marijuanos in Texas, Denver, LA even. This was how mota got to everyone back in the day. Not just good or way cheap Mexican, which at first was all there was. But then came sinsemilla, panama red, skunk. And then came the blow, the cocaína. I moved a lot more of the smoke, and yeah I partied too, but with OZ's of coke—small packages, riskier but tons easier—I banked really good too. I was smarter than I ever realized back then. It was why I had this house now. Kind of fucked up to say, but it was a good thing the band crashed when it did.

"That's what it got to be aquí, yeah," I told Gabriel. "Pero nací con el apellido. I'm born a *Cuevas*. That's my actual last name."

Gabriel took a few seconds, then he got it. "Jajaja! I understand! Ya entiendo lo que pasó! It only takes me a minute." Gabriel laughed more than it was worth. "Pero listen, mister..."

"Call me Jake. Jacobo está bien too, but Jake unless you really prefer Spanish."

"I want it inglés," he said. "Por favor. I try to use more de eso because I want it for my business to get big. I always want it for work in inglés, even when all my workers talk in espanish, me entiendes?"

I didn't entirely believe him—like maybe it was really about my pocho Spanish—but on the other hand, it did make a lot of business sense. Anglos have money, mexicanos don't. And white people don't like too many syllables for names. One syllable is best. Tom, Joe, Mike. Even Jerkoff, the name given to the gofer in our band back when the sky was always hilarious and blue, seemed like a one syllable to all somehow. Two syllables is their max for sure.

Gabriel was fast and he was strong. Like two men. He took pictures of where everything was on the walls—art my longest girlfriend collected for me—before he took anything down, winking and power fisting about his brains and abilities. He moved furniture to the center of my living room like they were trinkets. His son you could see wanted to help, but mostly he stayed on the sidelines, watching. He was good at running things down, like getting a thin plastic drop cloth that would cover all from splatter. But once opened, he couldn't seem to get the corner of the half his dad tossed him.

"Agárralo, Gabo!" he told his son impatiently. "Nada más hay que usar los dedos." He couldn't get his fingers to do what his dad's did easily though. Gabito wasn't going to be as big as his dad. His dad was husky and broad-shouldered, maybe six-three easy. He could've played American football. His son was skinny, fragile, wore glasses that seemed too big for his face.

"Sí sí, Papi," he said, but he was slow.

"Lemme help," I said moving in. Disabled, all and any moving was hard for me, sadly, but I didn't like not doing or trying to do what I once could.

"Dale las gracias al señor, Gabito," his dad told him as we spread the plastic.

"He doesn't need to thank me," I said.

"Gracias, Señor Caves," Gabito said obediently.

"In inglés! Talk En-ga-les!" Gabriel told him. "And este señor is called Mr Cuevas!" He said it strong, but all for fun, and he laughed for all of us.

"Gracias…thank you, Señor Cuevas," Gabito said.

His dad and I laughed.

"I am strict," Gabriel said. "I want my sons and daughters to show respect and to have courtesy to elders and to give thanks to God."

"You have high expectations. I am sure they will be met, too."

"You believe it is too much?"

"Oh no," I said. "I just say dumb shit." Isn't it a little hard to control all? Or that much, especially after a certain point. "You have four children?" Maybe he was more than thirty-five.

"Yes sir. And you?"

"Two girls. Women now, of course." That was not counting the son I had to pay for. I met and got to know him in his mid-twenties, and I wish I could say it was because of me that he turned out so well. Though I'd guess they aren't as fond of me, I love my girls.

All things in the middle of the room covered, Gabito, no words exchanged, brought him his paint tray and roller. And his dad went to a paint can with a screwdriver and popped the lid.

"God does the most, but we help, verdad?" Gabriel told me.

Ready for his next task, Gabito watched and listened, the lenses of his glasses distorting my own read of what he heard.

Listen to the winds and the floods, trees falling, trucks crashing into buses.

"Mande?" Gabriel said.

"What?" Yup, I did that again. "Nada nada, nothing," I said, shaking it off. "So where are you from, Gabriel?"

"Yo soy del mero Chihuahua," he exclaimed, then sang, "¡Que bonito es Chi hua *hua*!"

Proud to be from Chihuahua, and just as proud that he knew the lines from the song about the beauty of Chihuahua, he laughed a big wide laugh, and his son thought it was all the greatest.

"But I was born in a colonia near El Paso," he said, "y por eso I am americano like my son."

Gabito smiled big for that too.

"We are Villas!" he said, his roller hitting the wall. "¡Que vivan los Villa!"

"Pancho Villa?"

"El único y el mero mero."

"Wow, that is the best. Like...well, how close? From a brother or sister, or like through him, as a grandparent, great grandparent...that b word...Bisabuelo?"

"Por la sangre," he said firmly. "Our name, our blood. Verdad, mijo?" He was painting furiously, wanting to get the work done.

Skinny Gabito was looking right at me. His eyes as big as his great big papi.

Gabriel worked faster and harder in the living room and then he went into the two bathrooms and got them mostly done, but I had to tell him that eight p.m. was as late as he could stay and work. As much as I too wanted it finished as quick as possible, it's that I couldn't bear it into the late evening too. Though I did even less than Gabito, though I lived by myself, it made me tired and grouchy. I had no other place to go, my living room covered in a pile, and I could only be in my office so long. I'd expected another man working. And it's what he promised. He told me tomorrow, he'd have someone tomorrow, I shouldn't worry.

* * *

He was more on time the next morning, only a little more than an hour late. Almost two. He was alone again. With Gabito. I didn't believe it was about having another job waiting for him. What he needed was to get done and paid for all of it. It was that he'd said it would take two days, and he'd taken it hard that I brought that up the day before. He was determined to keep his word. Me, I just thought he needed another roller and brush besides his. I felt bad for him that he made the deal with me—I was torn between making him fulfill it and letting him off the hook and have four days even.

He was in the bedroom. He was going full blast. Gabito was near him, fidgeting, trying to seem busy. Gabito could only watch as his dad moved all in the room to the center, including that big bed and its wooden frame and a heavy chest of drawers and more. And it wasn't like I could do much, if anything, any more. Gabriel must have seemed as massive as the room to Gabito with or without those glasses. Close to the door, he moved with caution, he stayed still but at the ready, nervously motionless. Even I thought Gabriel had grown another inch or two up and in the shoulders overnight.

He brought it up. "My wife was supposed to come today. But she couldn't because..." He didn't finish.

He was talking to me without looking at me. And it suddenly flashed that his huge business was only his exuberance.

"My wife is better than most men," he said, turning to me. "And she has royal blood! She is a Juárez, a descendiente del presidente Benito Juárez."

"Wow, really?" I bought the Pancho Villa one without much thought, even though I'd heard that kind of claim before. It was something that people in El Paso say. And he'd been convincing. But she was family with Juárez?

"Isn't that right, Gabito?"

"Sí...yes, Papi."

"Where is she from?" I asked.

"Veracruz. All her family is there." His roller was rolling so much it sounded like it was breathing hard.

"But he was from Oaxaca," I said.

"Yes sir," he said without hesitation. "He was the president of all of Mexico and every Mexican. He was our greatest presidente. They say he did for los indios what Lincoln did for los negros aquí. No more slaves."

"And she has his blood," I said.

"What color you call that wood?" he asked of my chest of drawers.

"Walnut?" The question because it didn't connect.

"She is the color of walnut."

"Oh that proves it!"

I don't believe I said that out loud. Wasn't my intention. Neither of them said anything. Neither looked at me. Though they did get quiet. But if I did, they couldn't know I was being sarcastic.

"My wife can do many things," he said finally. "If you want, she can clean your house really clean. Every two weeks, a very good price. She has a business for cleaning."

"Maybe. What does she charge?"

"She will give you a good price." He winked and smiled as big as he was. "I know you, I think she knows me. I will get you a deal."

Hard when you have four children to do a business.

"Besides the most beautiful," he told me, "she's a strong woman. She is very intelligent, muy lista, and the best with business. She's maybe better than me! No, no lo crees, but I say so between us!"

Gabito laughed, happy. It was sweet and generous and bold like him. But I decided they were almost broke. I had nothing much to go on. Maybe his truck, a shiny Silverado. It didn't seem that old. Could be a year, could be ten. But I decided he was broke anyway.

I let him and Gabito do their work. I started thinking of people I knew who maybe needed painting or any work done by the giant mexicano y americano. I went to the Target and bought myself a new cheap watch and a band, and at the grocery store I bought a few extra apples and bananas, and then I stopped for a couple of burgers, fries, and sodas for them. I made sure I got back before lunchtime. Gabito was in his dad's truck, playing with the radio. The reggatón caught me by surprise.

"Caught ya!" I said. He did jump. He did something with the station.

"Oh hello, Señor Cuevas."

"I was just playing. Didn't mean to scare you."

He couldn't say anything,

"You hungry?" I said. "I got you and your dad a burger and fries."

"Oh thank you but we ate. My mom made us tacos to bring."

"And you already ate?" They never seemed to eat. "I bought cokes too. You don't want that either?"

He nodded for that.

"And fries? Eat fries?"

He thought they'd be okay too.

"I also got a few candy bars. For later maybe?"

That got bright eyes and a yes please grin.

"Thank you, Señor Cuevas."

Inside Gabriel couldn't be going faster. He had already moved the furniture into the center of the other bedroom and covered it.

"What I will do is paint this room with the flat, then I will do the semi-gloss. I will have your bedroom all done for you, no te preocupes, Mr Cuevas."

"Jake." Probably the walls didn't need second coats. So I'd let that go. My donation. "I bought burgers and fries, but Gabito says you both ate lunch."

"I can always eat!" He took both of the burgers. "Gabito never wants food. Nunca come, mi chamaco." He took a burger in one hand and rolled paint with the other.

I hid in my office to burn hours. The office was going to be the largest time hassle because of my book collection. My library, covering all four walls, and including a thick, decorative wooden shelf of books encircling the whole room. The interests in these books shocked and disoriented everyone. Because I'm an ex-musician, stoned and high all that time, and an ex-dealer. When did anyone ever see me read a book? Talk about a book? Express a complex idea or a profound question based on brains and wisdom, and not because of a psychedelic or even some shitty mota? I was clearly a stoopid who got lucky playing guitar in a band that got lucky for a decade of crazy fun and good bucks.

I didn't sit and play games on my computer. I say that in my defense. Though if I did maybe I wouldn't have heard Gabito's feet pacing up and down my hall. I don't know why, but my sense was that it wasn't what he was supposed to do, just all he could think of. It was late afternoon, very close to evening. I didn't hear his dad's voice much.

"Hey I got a job for you, Gabito." I wanted him to take the band off my new watch and put the other one on. I couldn't do it.

He opened the office door and his tiny black eyes behind those oversize frames flashed colors.

"Lots of books, huh?"

"Sí, muchísimos!" he said. "I never seen so much, Señor Cuevas."

He'd never been to a library?

"You must study a lot," he said.

I laughed, though I liked it and took it like it was a real compliment. "My daughters, they read a lot. In college."

He stepped in, looking at spines.

"You like to read?"

"Yes sir. Mostly comics, but..."

Gabriel was at the office door. He looked beat. The room, my office, the work still to come, I'd say when he saw it, it was if he'd just dropped a heavy barbell and was limp in his legs. "No molestes a Mr Cuevas, Gabo," he said as if he had caused what he saw.

"He's no bother! Not at all. He's just a smart boy who asked about all the books. And I was just telling him, most really comes from my girls. When they went to college, I paid for all these books. And then I bought them all back from them, better than selling them back to any bookstore. And then I kept them, like trophies, or souvenirs. Because I was proud of my girls and wanted them to know it, and how much their worthless dad loved them and what they did. And they are both super smart. But I did look inside them. I can't tell you all of them. My girls came and brought me learning like they were heaven's angels! I was amazed at all there was around me I hadn't seen or heard of, like I'd come from another planet. I learned about botany, astronomy, geography, mythology, México before the conquistadores, Africa, Rome, philosophy, poetry, art..."

And then I heard what I'd been saying, more than old or grumpy something out loud. Instead, I got so full of whatever it was, I'd become more like a street looney, preaching like I could spraken zie German, or Latin! Me, a wise gray beard German professoring, me in Catholic hat and vestments muttering sacred Latin—and here I really was, a scraggly old fuck, barefoot and crippled, jeans torn at the knees, a big oak god stick. And this made me, kind of suddenly, burst out laughing so hard I spit and sprayed it.

Gabriel and Gabito flinched but, polite, didn't show much more. God knows what they thought.

"This is what I think," I told Gabriel as I stood up, composing myself. "You finish what you're doing right now. I can try to get some of these books out into the hall for tomorrow. You go home, get some rest, and we'll get it tomorrow. It's all going good, turning out good, todo está saliendo excelente y tenemos mañana!" I waited but nothing came. "We'll get it all done tomorrow, right?"

Gabriel didn't say anything, just nodded his head yes, pumped a fist, and went to the main bedroom where he was finishing the semi-gloss work there.

Gabito wasn't sure what to do.

"You want to help me move some of these books? Helps your dad some too."

Not all were heavy hardbacks. Most weren't. I'd started collecting first editions too, and they weren't so heavy either. Novels, poetry books, histories of countries. A few in Spanish, German, French, none of which I could read. It had become a hobby of mine since I had to stop playing music. I liked the books with unAmerican names in the title. The poetry of Rumi. Nagarjuna and the middle way. Malintzin. Genghis Khan. Sor Juana. Al Ghazali and Maimonides. Cuauhtémoc. I'd found dictionaries in Sanskrit, Kurdish, and Persian! I thought all these were beyond cool. Gabito and I could carry about the same amount. I showed him how to stack them in the hallway so that I could put them back in the same places.

Seemed like I could take four at a time pretty easy. Gabito too.

"If we put them down así," I showed him, "then when we pick them up to put them back, they'll be in the same order.

And we set them down here in the hall, and then a new stack on the left of each."

He got it fast and we did a lot of the books, all that I could handle and reach.

"You want a candy bar?"

Of course he did. His favorite? Chocolate, any kind.

"Señor Cuevas," he said, "how did you hurt your legs and your arm? Because you played la guitarra? In a rock band?" He said "rock" like it was Spanish, *roc*.

"Good question." His dad had told him about me of course, I just hadn't even considered. So did I want to be careful and make it nothing, or did I want to shock him straight? Yeah, I was in a band, I started, when Gabriel came either incidentally because he'd finished, or because he could hear us talking all along. "I was pretty good enough at playing. And we were pretty popular and did a lot of gigs, which are places and shows. All over really, a lot here in Texas. And yeah of course we started getting pretty wild, too careless and out of control sometimes." They were both listening close. "Some nights we got ridiculous," I said for dad. "We were young, we felt like we had money, we weren't smart. We had a bus so we could go to a lot of gigs more comfortably. Anyway, one night we didn't know it—none of us paid any attention— but both our drivers—we had two—partied like they weren't supposed to, and got too messed up. Slammed us into an eighteen-wheeler at like four a.m. Two died. I rode in a wheelchair for months but here I am."

"Por las... because of drogas entonces, no?" said Gabriel.

I nodded, meaning probably. "And stupidity," I said.

I waited for more. He was not accidentally blurting out loud what he was thinking.

"So the rest tomorrow then?"

"Bueno, yes, that's good," he said. He took off down the hall.

Gabito had a few books that he wanted to move from and to and that was it for us.

I showed him my watch and asked if he could change bands for me. He stopped everything trying to get the old band off. I moved the last books to the hallway.

His dad yelled from the living room. "¡Gabo! ¡Ahorita! ¡Ven acá!"

Both feet were in the air moving before his dad stopped calling him.

I staggered to the living room as soon as I'd stacked the books Gabito didn't. There were still plenty, all the ones on the high shelf.

I got to the living room just as Gabriel barked "Andale, niño!! Agarre la esquina!!" It was the thin plastic drop cloth again. Gabito couldn't find his corner. It seemed to me he couldn't because he couldn't think straight because of his dad's impatient anger. Which he used to end the delay by yanking and dragging it across the mound of couches and furniture and then made a ball of all of it, pissed off. Then he started re-hanging all the little things and pics and art like he was beating an Olympics world time record. Done, he took on the toy furniture. It was almost like he picked up one end of a couch and carried by that end to where it was before the painting. Motionless, Gabito and I stared, out of his way but close enough in case of who knew what.

"So," I said when he was finished, "tomorrow."

"At 9, maybe more early," he said flat, exhausted.

"Vamos, Gabo. Mañana entonces, Mr Cuevas...Mr Jake."

They got here at almost 10. I didn't care. I wished him much
sleep the night before and into the morning. My only concern
was an appointment I had at 11:30. Gabriel went straightline
into my office. There was real heavy junk there aside from a
whole lotta fat books. A heavy wooden desk, heavy wooden
table, thick wooden bookcases, heavy chest of drawers also
wooden but full of every imaginable kind of paper, stuffed
over and under with thirty-five years of files. I decided to stay
far away. I sat on my couch, in my freshly painted living room.
So did Gabito, though he was clearly anxious about it, pacing
to the edge of the hall and peeking down, listening, where his
papi came in and out.

"You get breakfast?" I asked.

He nodded. "My mom made it for me, for all of us."

"Then you can have a candy bar because it's good, not because you're starving."

He was really skinny, but he ate that candy like it didn't
have to be so.

"Have another," I said tossing another. "What's your favorite?"

"Chocolate," he said like the word was Mexican.

"I meant which candy bar?"

"All. Any. I love them all if they are chocolate!"

That sounded like a boy from the same border I came up
on. I laughed, and he giggled like the kid he was, his brown
smeared teeth showing.

I had to get myself going. A bit more washing and comb-
ing, putting on some better shirt anyway for the dentist's office. Old as I was, I had to show good so nobody'd guess.

I was ready and passing by my office. Already all the books were off the high shelf, the shelves themselves stacked on my side table. He'd moved everything enough so he could reach the walls with roller and brush. It was way impressive.

"I'm on my way to see my dentist. I'll be back...in over an hour, maybe more."

His giant body was caught in a corner and he shoved the chest of drawers a few more inches so he could talk. "Perdón, Mr Jake," he said.

"Just Jake, Gabriel. Jake."

He nodded. He looked at me concerned. "I found this under that, on the floor." Stuck beside the heavy drawers, he handed me a photo.

"Fuck me!" I said loud and clear. I immediately wished only an accidental, unclear mumble. Because Gabito was right behind me, but also because of Gabriel's stern views. "That's Santa Chichona!" I said to explain my excitement. Another error of words before thoughts. But all I was saying was that I was happy he found it. "I thought it'd been stolen. It's that she used to be my girlfriend," I told him.

He furled his brow in near disbelief.

"You know, an old novia. Way long ago now."

"I found it on the floor, here." He pointed to what was probably the exact spot.

"All this time," I said, "and I'd thought it was stolen." I stopped. "Executed even by another girlfriend!" Me, I thought that line was pretty funny. He didn't. I think he saw me as a complete looney bird since the previous bursts of blather in my office. "Can't believe you found it," I said.

"She was your novia?" he asked. It was more statement dosed with disapproval.

It was kind of a hot photo. I meant, come on, you can't even smile about it? But he couldn't.

I went to my living room and sat. Here's the story: I used to have girlfriends even before marriage. I did pretty okay in that area, and then I was in a popular band, and there were more of them. My wife, who had her own talents and beauty, couldn't take it and baled. Girlfriends filled in. One was Ana, who the band called Santana because she was a Chicana who liked San Francisco. Ana was a strong woman, full of strange art talent, which was always overlooked because she was real cute. I'd gotten this house by then, for cheap I might add. And as a gift she brought me a nicho, a colorful Guadalupe-themed wood one, and she put a photo of herself in it. She was still mid-twenties young and oddly modest but she liked me, I liked her. She was busty, but she didn't flaunt it. Except in this photo. Standing, she held a slinky silk something to cover each nipple, her breasts under her crossed arms. Staring actually seemed more like sex than sexy. She insisted that I place it where every girl who visited me, with any scheming ideas, would see it and be warned. So they knew who my girl was. Very funny, right? We ended of course, and I moved that nicho onto the chest of drawers in my office. Everyone who came in was quick to see it and comment verbally or non-verbally. Women friends would shake their head. Call me perv. Say grow up. No matter what I explained, they'd go no, and say get rid of it. Men, of course, would stare. Most of them, though, would say they'd never be able to keep that around. I had a couple of girlfriends who agreed with not keeping it around strongly. One day I noticed it was gone. I was so used to it there, I didn't even notice when exactly it was not. It was just in my growing mess of things accumulating. The nicho there, the photo suddenly, or whenever, gone. My bet was probably Zelene who trashed it. That was her style, both as a jealous woman and a feminist lesbian.

I didn't know why I was so thrilled to have it back. How many years lost and mostly forgotten? At least twenty-five. A trophy? Maybe, but I really didn't think so, and not like the immediate thought. Sure it was sex. But it wasn't that. My young man past? Of course some. Memory? Sure. Not of her naked, her big boobs. Life that I had. That I lived. Full, then. Luckily then and I didn't realize it then. Before. Really. That because all I did and knew could sound like a big fish story. Whereas now I am an old looney tunes, talking shit and pedo. Talking to myself. Out loud, often by accident.

Where I would put it was in my office. A particular drawer. But I couldn't right then. I had to make my appointment. I slipped the photo under a straw place mat on the dining room table.

"Tell your dad I'll bring you both a couple burgers and fries on the way back—or would you rather me pick up burritos?"

"Okay Señor Cuevas. My papi always wants hamburgers most."

"I'll get him a double."

* * *

A little more than an hour and a half. "Hello hello," I said. I liked to go to the dentist. Like getting a massage.

"Hello Señor Cuevas," said Gabito. "I have something for you."

"I have burgers and fries for you guys. And a coke." I handed that to him first and he took it fast. "Take this big one and these big fries to your big dad."

He ran them over. I was sitting beside the coffee table. I bought myself a chicken burger and, hungry, I was already into that.

"He says thank you."

"Here's yours," I said. I held out the wrapped burger.

"No, no thank you, Señor Cuevas."

"What, you don't want a burger? I thought you said you did?"

"No, no, but thank you."

He was drinking the soda.

"You ate?"

"I'm fine, thank you."

"The fries anyway?"

He hesitated, considered, and then said okay.

"You can sit on that couch, Gabito." Seemed like he thought he couldn't. He sipped through the straw. He loved the fries.

"Tell me, honest. You don't like hamburgers?"

He was reluctant. "Honest?"

"Yes, honest."

He was thinking.

I was thinking of one of my daughters. I said, "You don't eat beef? Any meat?"

He stared at me.

"Between us," I decided to say.

"Sometimes I do. But I don't want to. I don't. My mom makes me beans, and I love beans, and corn, and green beans."

"And chocolate."

He smiled.

"I could've gotten you a chicken burger if it's just beef. I could have given you mine if I hadn't scarfed it down. I could have bought you a veggie burger. You had one of them?"

He shook his head.

"You get used to them, and they're good."

He listened.

"Lots are just like you. Smart ones, who like books, like you. You're gonna do good, you'll see. You wanna candy bar?" I knew it wasn't good for him, but he looked so hungry always.

His eyes said yes. I had a few in a bowl.

"Have another if you want. They're not very healthy, you know that. But if your dad or mom won't mind." That got me thinking. But I decided I shouldn't be asking more. "Maybe take one or two in to your dad?"

When he got back, he came close to me. "See, I finally get it. It was easier once I followed the paper."

"Wow, the instructions. Who would've thought anyone could ever read those? But you could. Thank you, Gabito."

He liked what I said. And he got comfortable in the living room where I was, hovering near, talking, seeming to think about pleasing me. And not his dad.

Gabriel entered. He was holding a paint can and paint tray, a roller and brush in that. "Gabo, go get el plástico and all in there ahorita now. To me, "I am finish, Mr...Jake. You look at what I've done. Make sure you're happy with all the work so you hire me again please."

"I am sure I will be happy," I said standing. I passed Gabito already hustling out with the drop cloth balled up and some tools. I was shocked that all the books were out of the hall, back in the office. I'd expected...I don't know...to supervise putting them back? The bookcases were all put back right, the thick decorative carved shelves were all in place. And all the books, so many heavy ones, were stacked in and on them, neatly. But I had no idea if they were in any kind of order because all the spine of every single book, lying flat or on standing, was facing the wall. All that showed were the edges, some deckled, most not. No one, including me, could see the title of a single book. It was, I will say, an interesting point of view. I'd never seen something like it before. Probably only people who boxed or unboxed books for a living, for a warehouse maybe, had ever thought of books piled up and placed this way.

I saw Gabito outside with a hose, washing off a brush. Gabriel was at my kitchen sink, a bar of soap in his hands. Even his hands were enormous. Maybe not if he was Serbian, for example, but for a Mexicano, giant.

"So," he said, "all good for you, you're happy...Jake? I think I always do good work as any company. And I can do whatever you need. Carpentry, plomería, even the yard you want that. I have men who can do anything you need."

"You are a Villa!" I said.

"¡Que viva Villa!" he said laughing.

He wanted to go home. He wanted it done and to be on their way. He was persuasive. I wanted that too. I wanted to fall asleep on my couch more than discuss the books. I reached for my wallet. "You don't take..."

"Cash," he interrupted.

Really I already knew he'd say that. I'd gone to the bank after the dentist and before the burgers. I counted it out. It was $50 more than his price, and I only had hundreds.

"I don't have..."

"A tip. Keep it. Buy dinner for you both, for all maybe." I was thinking veggie burgers.

He was out, gratefully, to his Silverado. I wanted to wave bye to Gabito, but too much, and I turned the other way and hit the couch.

* * *

I fell asleep after maybe an hour and loved it. Loved the fresh paint in the living room I woke up in. Went to my bedroom and my bathroom and they were freshly painted and wasn't all this a good idea and why did I wait so long. I went to my office and thought oh my god, these books. I'd really have to think what I would have to do—a lot of work I couldn't do myself. I did like that it was painted. Never had been all these years. I shouldn't have let him go without doing it right. But it was also so crazy strange looking. I'd take pics. Nobody'd believe it. Wasn't it a perfect image of these times or my times?

This made me think of my Ana pic. That made me smile. I could not explain why. Because it was funny? Yes it was! Because it was sex and sexy? Okay, yes. I do still like women, I'm still a man, and how can I say I don't and why should I? Because I found it, or it was found. Meaning it was real, not something I imagined. All of it, her, everything I don't ever talk about, any of what was, to anyone. But I have me, myself, and sometimes I need to be sure my memories aren't just imaginary.

When I looked under the straw mat on the coffee table it wasn't there. I looked under the other mat. I looked on the floor nearby. I looked under the mat again. I shook the mat and the other mat. I got on the floor and looked under the couch. I moved the couch, dragged it out so the entire floor

where it was could be seen. I sat. I had not taken it to my bedroom or office.

I remembered Gabito nervously hovering close when I got
back from the dentist. I'd forgotten about the photo when I
got back. I was near the coffee table. And he was too. Nervous
with me.

He was a growing boy with growing urges. I thought about
that for a bit. I wanted the photo back, and the fact that I did
made me feel like I was about twelve or thirteen. I could call
Gabriel. I could mention the books. No, just tell him. I could
maybe offer to pay him. I would offer to pay him to help me
turn the books around. I called him.

"Una cosa más, one little thing. You know that photo?
Mi novia? It's gone. Lost again. I was thinking, can you ask
Gabito if he can think of where I put it?"

He spoke away from the phone speaker.

"He says no," Gabriel said a few seconds later.

"Okay, bueno, gracias."

"I can come by next week one day," he said.

I said sure.

In the band days, the craziest ones, I don't know where this
came from, but it made us laugh when we were most wiped
out. *We chew and we screw and then we die.* I can't explain
why I thought of that.

At first I felt robbed not having that photo I hadn't
cared about for so many years. Or ever, really, as a matter
of fact. Which made me smile and feel looney tunes like the
wrong-way books did. I laughed out loud. Nobody but me
heard: Gabito got his first nicho.

Peking Ducks

"SLAUSON," SHERRY SAID. "DOESN'T THAT SOUND... maybe Watts, like that, to you?"

"What?" Javi said making the word shorter than it already was.

"Slauson's kind of a ghetto name, right?"

Javi might have looked up and away irritated if he wasn't driving her car. Slauson was the street they were on, wide and industrial, gigantic warehouses and big rigs. It wasn't picturesque, that was true.

"I just don't know where we're going, that's all," she said. "I don't know this side of LA. You know that."

Javi said nothing.

"Don't get so mad at me all the time," Sherry said. "It just makes me a little uncomfortable being here. I'm sorry."

"It's not Watts," he told her. He'd lived in too many LA neighborhoods, all of them not like hers.

"Well I've just never been there. For all I know, it's where we are. I don't mean to sound... what I probably sound like to you. I'm only trying to be honest."

"We're going to a Mexican joint," Javi said, "and it'll have good food."

"You think?"

This time he did look over at her.

"I really am hungry," she told him.

He didn't believe her and didn't hide it. But it wasn't a neighborhood to meet for an early dinner. For any time, for a going out restaurant to exist, even a Mexican one. Strange to find any food whatever here.

"My dad has good taste," Javi said. He didn't really know if that was true. He barely knew the man except that he was his dad.

She thought she laughed to herself silently. He didn't say a word out loud either, but he heard the laugh and it pissed him off.

"You really have to stop," he told her. "Really, and now. Please don't be an ass...I haven't seen my dad in a long time, and I want to." He only ever saw his after a long time.

"I'm sorry. Honest." She wanted to sound casual. "Why so long?"

"He's always in Mexico. Or not here in LA. Until now."

"But back and forth, right?"

"Long story," he said. One he didn't really know.

She decided not to stay on that topic. It didn't sound up and up to her. She didn't understand why it could be such an unexplored subject.

"We should be close," he said. "Just keep looking."

"It's not about being in a Black neighborhood," she said defensively. "It's the poverty...you know what I mean."

"And you'd feel the same if it were Mexicans."

She shook her head at him. "You're trying to fight."

"Okay, it's me," Javi said sarcastically. "Please keep your eye out. It's called Las Delicias de Mexico. Should be really close."

"Yum, delicious," Sherry said.

"No, *delicias*," he corrected, petty. Then, "There it is."

The restaurant, painted red, was on a big corner lot, as much dirt as gravel, old cars and pickups parked around it by natural rules, with no lines. A morena in a white peasant blouse holding a platter was part of a neon sign, not lit up because it was still sunny out, not even close to getting dark. The structure didn't seem like something built as a restaurant. An office building? Small warehouses were beside on both its sides.

Sherry wanted to tell him to park carefully. To lock her car. It wasn't even a two-year-old, shiny Toyota, way out of place here. But she didn't.

Out of the car, Javi scanned where they were . "Really is a pretty strange-looking restaurant, isn't it?"

Uncomfortable about too much, she didn't know what she could say.

The entrance was through a plywood, once glass, door. Inside, booths circled the room, with tables in the center, and only a few patrons. A TV on a countertop was tuned to a local Mexican station, loud only because it was like closing hours quiet in there. An older Mexican lady saw them and immediately disappeared until out popped a young waitress who stopped herself from speaking in Spanish. She led them to a windowed booth near the TV.

"Is here good?" she asked.

"Perfecto," Javi said. "Esperamos a uno más. Mi padre. Thank you."

"Ohh! Un momentito," and she went off to the back.

"What is that?" Sherry said like it couldn't wait, though she was trying to point subtly. "Aren't those ducks?" The bird carcasses were hanging on wires behind the countertop and continued around the corner into the hallway.

Javi hadn't seen them and never had before either.

"In Spain," she said, "restaurants might have hams, you know, for jamón serrano..."

Javi had never seen hanging hams, never been to Spain, never saw skinned chickens or ducks tied up bronzed and dead in any restaurant in LA.

"Hello," a voice spoke where they weren't looking. Neither of them had noticed the small man approach. "You must be the son of Margarito Sánchez." He paused like he had to organize his words before he went on. "Those are Peking ducks," he said, his laugh bursting out. Startling, it was that its depth just didn't match his height. He was Asian. "A Mexican delicacy!" He laughed again. His huge voice really didn't go with his weight either. "I am Mr Lee." He held out his hand to Javi. "I am the owner here. My restaurant is this."

Javi stood as best he could in the booth to politely acknowledge Mr. Lee and introduced Sherry.

"Your father, he is very good man. He work for me maybe ten years now."

"Here?" Javi blurted out. He meant the restaurant, though it may as well have been anywhere. Because he never really understood what his dad did or where. His mom wouldn't even try to tell him—who knows, she'd snip—if she knew ever. It wasn't here, he didn't have to ask.

"En México," Mr Lee said in well-enunciated Spanish. "I have too much business that comes from there to here," he said, back in less fluent English.

Javi was about to ask more but Sherry was faster.

"You raise and sell Peking ducks?"

Though it wasn't clear if she was joking, Mr Lee laughed his big laugh. "I sell those here. I am very good at them. They are the best!"

"Here," she asked. "At this, at...at your Mexican restaurant? Peking duck, with refried beans and rice?"

"That is a good idea, very good idea," he boomed. He laughed for all inside, which was almost nobody, the two of them going along with it, smiling. "My wife, la señora que...the lady that you meet first, she make this restaurant. She is from Oaxaca, she is the best cook, the very best. You can taste it when you eat." He stopped this line of talk. "Your papá is usually on time."

Javi nodded.

"He want me to meet you. Javier, that's it? He said que te interesa un jale...que...you want to work en México."

"Yes, that's true, I did. I do." Surprised, Javi answered even though he hadn't ever suggested it. Maybe he'd said something about going to Mexico to him on the phone once, long ago, but for sure no hint of it came up the other night when they talked, on the phone, when he said to meet him here. Javi almost never talked to his dad, maybe once every year, at best, usually not much when they did. Neither of them could talk comfortably, directly—and it was always on the phone—he was actually ever with him only twice. Now he'd come to see his dad. It'd been years. He was sixteen or seventeen the last time. This was something. He wanted to come.

"We have to talk then. I have to tell you. Or maybe your papá already said?"

Sherry's face showed more than Javi's.

"He didn't say anything to me, no. But I would love to hear what...whatever it is you do. The work. I'm interested."

"Bueno, okay. But first you eat. Your papá is late but first you eat. Wonderful food here, you see. Have ice tea, or beer." Mr Lee got up. "All free, no charge. My gift. I get you service." He went off.

"So what was that about?" Sherry said. "You want to work for him? Or just go to Mexico?"

"Maybe," Javi said.

"Might've been nice to let me in on your plans."

"Hey, I didn't know."

"You could've told me before we came. It would've been—"

"I didn't plan anything about it!"

"—I probably would've been fine," she finished. "Just a lot less mysterious."

"We came to see my dad. That's why we came. That was it."

She didn't believe him. It showed in her angry blush. She couldn't imagine them talking so little when they talked, how casually they'd come here to meet this father he never saw, and at this restaurant of all places. To catch up. Out of almost nowhere.

"And here we are," she said. "Kinda crazy."

He couldn't explain and didn't try.

The waitress brought them chips and a thick red salsita and two menus. They each ordered a beer. They both were reluctant to talk.

"If she's from Oaxaca, I bet the mole is really good," Sherry said. Besides Spain, she'd been to Mexico, too. Javi didn't know anything about Oaxaca or mole except the kind that came from jars bought at some Mexican bakery that had grocery things too. "They're the best there," she said. "Known for it. It's where moles were invented I think. Well, maybe not 'invented'..."

"I'm getting some tacos," Javi said, setting the menu down.

"We could go to Mexico," she said. "Together." She set her menu on the table. "You'll have to try my mole. You'll love it."

He nodded, meaning yeah right maybe.

"Save a little money, figure out how much time there." She waited for his response. "You've really never been?"

"If Tijuana counts. Got car upholstery there. Twice. It was good too. A lot cheaper."

"Funny how that is," she said. "I've been and you haven't."

The wooden entrance door opened and the square of light flashed like a firecracker. Javi's father. Not tall, not short, was a husky, well-formed man. He was wearing boots, jeans that were clean, even pressed, a shirt so white it seemed like it was a bright color, while his skin was so dark it was hard to see his face against the bright light coming through the window. He shook hands with his son at a distance that was his, firmly, strong, like he might pull him from the booth. Introduced to Sherry, he shook her hand more gently, kind.

"I'm sorry I'm late," he said. Almost hard to hear, the volume of his voice especially low in contrast with Mr Lee's.

They listened for more.

"Did you order?" he asked.

"We said we'd wait."

"The best food here."

"We met Mr Lee," Javi said.

"Good. His wife is the cook."

"I love your linen shirt," Sherry said. It was a pullover, three buttons at the neck, collarless.

Javi's father was surprised by the compliment, or that she called it linen. "It looks nice, I think. It's from Mexico. Popular there."

"Comfortable too," Sherry said.

"Yes, exactly."

"From Oaxaca?"

He thought. "Or Veracruz," he said. "I don't remember."

"Is that where you live, or Oaxaca?" she asked. "Or was it Morelos?" She looked at Javi asking that. He'd told her that's where he lived.

The waitress interrupted with a menu for Javi's dad. She asked him if he wanted a beer. He said sí, porfa.

"We're ready to order," Sherry told the waitress. "I'm so hungry," she told Javi. "All this talk about how good the food is!" she told both of them.

She ordered pollo en mole negro and Javi tacos de carne asada. His father said he'd have the same as him.

"One of us should have gotten the Peking duck with rice and beans plate," Sherry said.

Javi's father didn't follow.

"It's because of the ducks hanging right there," Javi told him.

Javi's dad looked at the line of large birds unsurprised.

"He told her he doesn't serve them here," Javi said.

Javi's dad laughed. "It's one of his movidas...his businesses I think. In the States."

Quiet but for the TV. It was like neither son or father could talk, while Sherry had a thousand curiosities. "So," she said, "you are friends with Mr Lee. And you work for him?"

"Yes," Javi's dad said.

"In Mexico? Or here, in the US?"

"Mostly there."

"In Oaxaca?"

He nodded. Then, "Not only. A lot though..." It seemed like he would say more.

Javi was trying to let all her questioning run out, but he couldn't take anymore. "Give it a rest, Sherry," he said.

Sherry almost spoke anyway but Javi's dad spoke first.

"He is from there. The first chinito ever born there." He smiled at Javi. "I don't know if the first, but they say this about him. He's a mexicano, can you believe that." He laughed quietly.

Javi gladly laughed with his dad.

"I like him," Javi's dad said. "He does a lot better than all of us."

Sherry said, "I learned that native Mexican people and Native Americans are probably from Asia. They crossed the Bering Straits." She caught herself. "Not plural I don't think. Bering Strait."

Neither of them said anything. They both sipped their beers. The other patrons were already gone or leaving. It got too quiet until a few LAPD cruisers screaming by with sirens filled the space.

"I'm just too curious where you live," Sherry announced. "I can't help myself," she told Javi.

Javi's dad leaned to see out the left side of the window better. "I am living in a casita allá, over there." That's when he saw, they all saw, the flume of smoke near where he was pointing. "It belongs to Mr Lee."

"Is that a fire?" Javi said. "Looks like after a bomb drops."

It was whirl of white smoke mushrooming, like a slow swerving top, curling on its sides.

"Kind of beautiful," Sherry said. "If it's not...some tragedy. I don't think it's industrial, do you?"

"It's very close to the casita," Javi's dad said, worried.

The waitress came with the plates of food. Right behind her Mr Lee rushed in. "Hay un incendio!" he told Javi's dad instead of saying hello. He was at the TV changing stations. Nobody at the table paid too much attention to the food, not even the waitress who went immediately to the window in the next booth to see better.

"Do you want to go see?" Javi asked his dad.

Javi's dad didn't answer.

Mr Lee found an English-language station, filming live.[1] The news reporter was hiding beside a house near the one on fire. There was gunfire and police uniforms of several kinds, LAPD swat team and fire trucks in every other TV shot. They were trying to capture the SLA, the Symbionese Liberation Army, and in a fog of tear gas they were encountering rounds from automatic weapon coming from inside the burning house. The SLA had robbed and shot a store owner of a sporting goods store not far away in Inglewood the day before.

"Patty Hearst!" Sherry exclaimed. "They're going to kill her!"

---

1. On May 17, 1974, the Symbionese Liberation Army, a radical leftist organization who had kidnapped heiress Patty Hearst, got into a shootout with the Los Angeles Police Department. Besides the fire, six SLA members were killed.

Mr Lee stood a couple of feet from the TV. The other three fidgeted at their table, going from watching TV to the smoke outside.

"How far away is it?" Javi asked his dad.

"Not very far," his dad said. "A mile. Less. Nomás cuadras de aquí." He got up and stood beside Mr Lee.

He must have said something to him because Mr Lee said, in his normal loud voice. "Mejor que no hasta que... pues ay está!" he said when there was a scroll on the screen. "Están en la East 54th."

Javi's dad said something else not audible.

"Un horror," Mr Lee said, "pero no está tan cerca de la casa."

"Que bueno," Javi's dad said turning toward the table. He got himself one of his tacos.

"Do you know who they are?" Javi asked. "They've been in the news here a while, a lot."

"Americanos," he said, a little joking. "Crazy gringos, que no?"

"Kinda, yeah," Javi said, smiling.

"No hay locos donde vivimos," Mr Lee said. The two older men laughed. "Nada más culos y pendejos y a veces un puta madre o dos." This time three of them laughed harder. The older two of them stepped aside and talked.

Coming back to stand by the table, Javi's dad grabbed another of his tacos. "You guys eat. We're going to the house to be sure all is good. You eat the good food. I'll be a little time away. Not much, okay?"

Javi didn't answer fast because he wanted to go with them. He figured Sherry was why he couldn't. "Sure," he said, disappointed.

The TV was full of the sound of automatic rifle shots, spraying, the reporter said, from the basement of the house, tear gas and smoke billowing out. From the restaurant window, they could see black smoke swirling into a taller and fuller plume of white. Besides two silent patrons who ate watching the TV from a few tables away, and the waitress half cleaning tables, half watching TV, it was just Javi and Sherry. Neither ate their food.

"I think we should go," Sherry said.

"My dad says they'll be right back."

"I think they're closing," she said. "No, they are closing."

"It's early," he said. "Why would they close?"

"They close early here every day. It's a breakfast and lunch restaurant."

"How do you know that?"

"It's what the sign says." She pointed. It was in a window near the entrance, easily read even if the hours faced the street.

"Do you want to try the mole?" she asked while he thought.

"Not right now."

"It is really great," she said softly, to herself mostly, to sound and feel calm.

More police cars, sirens wailing, screamed past the window. A fury of gunshots on the TV. The live reporter was whispering from hidden positions, and then softly yelling into his microphone.

"I really think we should leave," Sherry told him.

He didn't reply. He wasn't even looking at her.

"Javi, I want to leave."

"But he said to wait."

"I want to leave, Javi. I mean it."

He sighed at her.

She got her purse and put it on her lap. "I don't want to be sitting here waiting until it's really dark."

"They'll be back."

"I'm uncomfortable," she said. "I want to go." She got out of the booth.

"Yeah," he said.

"We can't know when they'll get back anyway. They could get stuck. Who knows?"

"Okay okay," he conceded. He got up. He asked the waitress if there was a bill and she said no. Sherry left six ones on their table anyway. An ambulance and two fire trucks passed as they both got into her Toyota. He headed the other way from the scene, west on Slauson toward the Harbor Freeway.

"Whoa," Sherry said relieved. "I'm ready to be home."

He didn't say anything. He couldn't find live news on the AM band of the radio and he went back to FM.

"Are you okay?" she asked.

"Yeah, sure."

"You don't seem all right."

"I shouldn't even have thought of doing the freeway," he said. It was moving like 30 mph at best. Southbound seemed stopped.

"We couldn't just sit there," she said.

"My dad said they'd be right back."

"I was really uncomfortable, Javi."

"You said. We left. It's done, it's cool."

"I guess I was scared, honestly."

He didn't reply.

"You're mad at me."

"No."

"Yeah you are."

"I wanted to stay longer."

"But what if they didn't come back?"

"They would've."

"When though?"

"Okay, you're right."

"I'm sorry about how I felt."

"We left, it's done."

"I was...uncomfortable."

"It's all right. I understand."

"Thank you," she said to him sweetly. "I know you wanted time with your dad."

He didn't say anything.

"It was good, really interesting, until all that happened."

He turned up the volume for "Superstition." They didn't talk. They were moving onto the Santa Monica Freeway, which had even worse traffic.

"I liked your father," Sherry said once Stevie Wonder finished singing. "He's handsome. Like you."

He didn't say anything.

"Easy to see why your mom..."

"Don't go there," he told her.

She waited.

"You can call him? We can do it again."

He nodded.

She assumed the traffic wasn't helping anything. "I wonder what we would have done, you know, if not the...SLA. Do you think we would have gone over to his place? Mr Lee's...casita?"

He didn't say anything.

"I don't know why you're so mad. Or is it just me?"

He glanced over at her. A little longer this time because they were in the stop of the stop-and-go slog. "Let it go, all right?"

They were a couple exits away. "Are you still thinking about going to Mexico?"

He nodded. "Seems like a good time."

"Why?"

"Because I'm young still."

"If it's to work, too, don't you need to know...you don't even know what it is your father does for a living."

"What's that supposed to mean, Sherry?"

"Nothing! Just normal...maybe I don't know," she said. "It just seems like nothing's clear enough. Even Mr Lee. Your mom won't even talk about your dad or..."

"Leave my mom out of this!" He'd raised his voice, which he didn't do much. "And you don't know me either."

"You don't know you," she shot back, mad. "You don't know what you're doing."

They were finally exiting.

"I'm sorry," she said. "I'm sorry. It's just Friday traffic. This day is like...full moon nuts. Those ducks!"

He didn't say anything. He was as quiet as his dad.

He found a parking space close to her West LA apartment. Where she lived was really nice. Better than any place he'd ever lived. She was really generous, smart. It was new to Javi, she was, her life was, all of it. They'd been seeing each other for about two years, and, aside from job time, he was with her almost always.

On the sidewalk she stopped for him. "What?" she said.

"Your car keys," he said.

She took them and stepped toward her apartment.

He didn't move.

"What?" she said.

"I'm going back there." His car, an older Pontiac, was parked on the street a block away.

"There? It's closed, Javi!"

He didn't say anything.

"You're not going back there."

She stared at him, he didn't look at her.

"Okay then," she said. She saw a crescent moon on the horizon above him, the oddly beautiful light all around them seeming to come from behind it, though it wasn't.

He started walking to his car.

"Like you think you're going to Mexico," she said more loudly.

He went. And he never did go back to West LA.

Also by Dagoberto Gilb

A Passing West
Mexican American Literature: A Portable Anthology
Before the End, After the Beginning
The Flowers
Hecho en Tejas: An Anthology of Texas Mexican Literature
Gritos
Woodcuts of Women
The Last Known Residence of Mickey Acuña
The Magic of Blood
Winners on the Pass Line